PU
Ed

NIGHT BIR

Many years ago, late in the middle watch of a calm winter's night, a square-rigged, three-masted ship, the *Sarah Casket* was making her way slowly through northern seas. Frost glimmered on the ship's white deck and tinselled her shrouds; long icicles sometimes fell chiming from the spars to the planks beneath.

And on the deck a child lay sleeping in a wooden box, so still and pale that she seemed more like a wax doll than a human being. It was Dido Twite, and she had been asleep for more than ten months. (Dido was missing, presumed dead, at the end of *Black Hearts in Battersea*, but it would take more than shipwreck to finish a girl like her.)

Suddenly the lookout yelled from the crosstrees, 'Whale-o! Dead ahead, not more'n a mile!' and Dido woke at last, only to find that she was aboard one of the strangest vessels that ever sailed the seas. There was the poor melancholy widowed captain, scouring every ocean in search of a pink whale, his frightened little daughter Penitence Casket, who had locked herself in a cabin and wouldn't come out, and the mate, a suspicious-looking character whose name was Slighcarp. There was also a mysterious veiled lady hiding in the blubber room. In short, the ingredients for a really big adventure, one that threatened yet again to topple the very throne of England, and Dido and Penitence with it.

This is Joan Aiken's third fantasy in Puffins; it is as deliciously outrageous as ever, and her own enjoyment of her characters and story just as apparent. It is warmly recommended for readers of ten and over.

The Wolves of Willoughby Chase, *Black Hearts in Battersea*, *The Whispering Mountain*, *The Cuckoo Tree*, *A Small Pinch of Weather*, *All But a Few* and *The Kingdom Under the Sea* are also available in Puffins.

JOAN AIKEN

Night Birds on Nantucket

ILLUSTRATED FROM DRAWINGS
BY PAT MARRIOTT

PUFFIN BOOKS

Puffin Books, Penguin Books Ltd,
Harmondsworth, Middlesex, England
Penguin Books Australia Ltd, Ringwood, Victoria, Australia
Penguin Books Canada Ltd, 41 Steelcase Road West,
Markham, Ontario, Canada

—

First published by Jonathan Cape 1966
Published in Puffin Books 1969
Reprinted 1972, 1975
Copyright © Joan Aiken, 1966
Illustrations copyright © Jonathan Cape Ltd, 1966

—

Made and printed in Great Britain by
Cox & Wyman Ltd,
London, Reading and Fakenham
Set in Monotype Garamond

N

NANTUCKET

MADAKET
HARBOUR

BRANT POINT
LIGHT

NANTUCKET
TOWN

ATLANTIC OCEAN

GREAT
POINT
LIGHT

WAUWINET

NANTUCKET HARBOUR

SACHACITO
POND

SANKATY
HEAD
LIGHT

POLPIS

SOUL'S
HILL

X

HIDDEN
FOREST

CASKET
FARM

SIASCONSET

CONTENTS

I

On board the Sarah Casket *– the sleeper wakes –
tale of the pink whale – half a world from home*

LATE in the middle watch of a calm winter's night, many
years ago, a square-rigged, three-masted ship, the *Sarah
Casket*, was making her way slowly through northern seas,
under a blaze of stars. A bitter, teasing cold lurked in the
air; frost glimmered on the ship's white decks and tinselled
her shrouds; long icicles sometimes fell chiming from the
spars to the planks beneath. No other sound could be heard
in the silent night, save, from far away, the faint barking
of seals.

On the deck a child lay sleeping in a wooden box filled
with straw. Sheepskins covered her warmly. Had it not
been for her breath, ascending threadlike into the Arctic
air, she would have seemed more like a wax doll than a
human being, so still and pale did she lie. Near by squatted
a boy, hunched up, his arms round his knees, gravely
watching over her. It was his turn below, and by rights
he should have been in his bunk, but whenever he had
any time to spare he chose to spend it by the sleeping
child.

She had been asleep for more than ten months.

Presently a bell rang and the watches changed. Bearded
sailors came yawning on deck, others went below; one, as
he passed the boy, called out:

'Hey, there, Nate! No sign of life yet, then?'

The boy shook his head without replying.

One or two of the men said:

'Why don't you give over, boy? She'll never wake in
this world.'

And one, a narrow-faced character with close-set eyes and a crafty, foxy look to him, said sourly:

'Why waste your time, you young fool? If it weren't for you and our sainted captain she'd have been food for the barracootas long ago.'

'Nay, don't say that, Mr Slighcarp,' somebody protested. 'She've brought us greasy luck so far, hain't she? We're nigh as full with whale-oil as we can hold.'

'Hah!' sneered the man called Slighcarp. 'What's *she* to do with the luck? We'd have had it whether we picked her up or no. I say she'd be best overboard before it changes. I've allus hated serving on a chick frigate.'

He went below, muttering angrily. Meanwhile the boy, Nate, calmly and taking no notice of these remarks, addressed himself to the sleeping child.

'Come on now, young 'un,' he said. 'It's your suppertime.'

One or two of the men lingered to watch him as he carefully raised the child with one arm and then, tilting a tin coffee-pot which he held in the other hand, poured down her throat a thick black mixture of whale-oil and molasses. She swallowed it in her sleep. Her eyelids never even fluttered. When the pot was empty Nate laid her down again in her straw nest and replaced the sheepskins.

'Blest if *I'd* care to live on such stuff,' one of the men muttered. 'Still and all, I guess you've kept her alive with it, Nate, eh? She'd have been skinny enough by now, but for you.'

'Guess I like looking after live creatures,' Nate said mildly. 'I'd been a-wanting summat to care for ever since my bird Mr Jenkins flew away in the streets of New Bedford. And Cap'n Casket says there's no more nourishing food in this world than whale-oil and m'lasses. Ye can see the young 'un thrives on it, anyways; six inches she've grown since I had the feeding of her.'

'And for what?' snarled the first mate, the foxy Mr

Slighcarp, reappearing from the after-hatchway. 'What pleasure is it for us to see our vittles vanishing down that brat's throat when, so far as anyone can see, it's all for Habakkuk? Break it up, now, men! Those that's going below, *get* below!'

The men were dispersing quickly when a cry from aloft galvanized them in a different way.

'Blo-o-ows! Thar she *blows*!'

The lookout in the crosstrees was dancing up and down, dislodging, in his excitement, about a hundredweight of icicles which came clanking and tinkling to the deck. His arm was extended straight forward.

'Whale-o! Dead ahead, not more'n a mile!'

And indeed on the horizon a pale silvery spout of water could just be seen.

Like ants the men scurried about the ship while Mr Slighcarp shouted orders.

'Set royals and t'gallants! Bend on stuns'ls! Lower the boats!'

Light as leaves, three long cedarwood whaleboats glided down from the davits on to the calm sea. But just before the boats were manned a startling thing occurred. As if roused by all the commotion, the child lying in her straw-filled box turned, stretched, and yawned, drawing thin hands from under the sheepskin to knuckle her still-shut eyes. The boy Nate had gone below, but one of the sailors running by noticed her and exclaimed:

'Land sakes to glory! Look at the supercargo! She's stirring! She's waking!'

'Devil's teeth, man! Never mind the scrawny brat now! See to the boats!'

Thus urged, the men swung nimbly to their places in the boats, but they went with many a backward look at the child who was moving restlessly now under the pile of sheepskins, still with her eyes tight shut. Waves of colour passed over her pale face.

But the boats had sped away, hissing in white parallels over the dark sea that was like a great rumpled black-and-silver patchwork quilt, before the child finally opened her eyes and struggled to a sitting position.

She looked about her blankly. All was still now on board the whaler. Even with the added canvas the ship made but slow headway in that light air and the boats had long drawn ahead. Only a few shipkeepers remained on board and they were occupied elsewhere.

The child stared vaguely about her until at length her eyes began to fix, with puzzled intelligence, on the few things visible in the dim light from a lantern hanging over her head. She could see white-frosted planking, a massive tangle of rigging between her and the stars, a dark bulk, the try-works, amidships, and above the gleam of spare tools lodged on the skids.

'This ain't the *Dark Dew*,' she murmured, half to herself. 'Where can I be?'

The boy, Nate, was passing at that moment. When he heard her voice he started, nearly dropping the mug he carried. Then he turned and cautiously approached her.

'Well I'll be gallied!' he breathed in amazement. 'If it isn't the Sleeping Beauty woke up at last!'

The child stared at him wonderingly and he stared back at her. He saw a girl who might have been nine or ten, with a pointed face and long tangled brown hair hanging over her shoulders. She saw a thin boy of about sixteen, hollow-cheeked and with eyes set so deep that it was impossible to guess their colour.

'*You* aren't Simon,' she said wonderingly. 'Where's Simon?'

'Human language, too! Who's Simon?'

'My friend.'

'There's no Simon on board this hooker,' the boy said, squatting down beside her. 'Here, want a mug o' chowder?

It's hot, I was just taking it to the steersman – he's my uncle 'Lije. But you might as well have it.'

'Thank you,' she said. She seemed dreamy, still only half awake, but the hot soup roused her. 'What's your name?' she asked.

'Nathaniel Pardon. Nate, they call me. What's yours?'

'Dido Twite.'

'Dido – that's a funny name. I've heard of Dionis – never Dido. You're British, ain't you?'

'Of course I am,' she said, puzzled. 'Ain't you?'

'Not me. I'm a Nantucketer.' And he sang softly:

'Oh, blue blows the lilac and green grows the corn
And the isle of Nantucket is where I was born,
Sweet isle of Nantucket! where the plums are so red,
Ten hours and twelve minutes south-east of Gay Head.'

'Never heard of it,' Dido said. 'What ship's this, then?'

'The *Sarah Casket*, out of Nantucket.'

'Did you pick me up?' she asked, knitting her brows together painfully in an effort to recall what had happened.

'Sure we picked you up, floating like a bit o' brit. And from that day to this you've lain on the deck snoring louder'n a grampus; *I* never thought you'd trouble to wake up. You seemed all set to sleep till Judgement. Cap'n Casket allowed as how you musta had a bang on the head, maybe from a floating spar, to knock you into such an everlasting snooze. You musta had considerable dreams all that time, didn't you?'

'Dreams?' she murmured, rubbing her forehead. 'I can't remember . . . The ship caught fire and me and Simon was in the sea, hanging on to a spar. Then he was on a rock . . . You're sure you didn't pick up a boy called Simon?'

'No, honey,' he said gently.

'Maybe some other ship did.' Dido was still hopeful. 'When'll we get to port?'

''Bout eight months from now. Maybe nine.'

15

'Eight *months*? Are you crazy? There ain't that much sea atwixt England and Hanover.'

'That's not where we're bound, chick. Back to Nantucket, that's where we'll be heading, soon's our casks are all full. That'll set you a step on your way, anyhows. Guess you can find some packet out o' New Bedford that'll take you to England.'

Plainly these names meant nothing to Dido.

'Where are we now, then?' she asked.

'Somewhere north o' Cape East. Just to raise another whale or two and we'll be homeward bound. Then all the casks'll be full.'

'Full of what?'

'Spermaceti o' course – whale-oil. What d'you think you've been living on for the last ten months?'

'Ten months? I've been aboard this ship for *ten months*?'

'Guess so. And pretty scrawny you'da been by now if I hadn't kept pouring whale-oil and sulphur and m'lasses down your gullet.'

Dido looked quite dazed. 'Ten months,' she repeated, half to herself. 'How did you come to pick me up, then? Where was it?'

For the first time the boy Nate appeared slightly embarrassed. 'Well,' he explained hesitantly, 'we was a mite off course. It was this how, you see. Cap'n had fixed to go after sperm-whales in the western grounds, so we was a-cruisin' off Madeira. And then the Old Man – he's a fine captain, just old pie on knowing where they're running, could raise you a whale in a plate o' sand, but he's funny in one way, awful peculiar – '

He stopped, his mouth open.

'Go on,' said Dido. 'How's he funny?'

A voice from behind made her start.

'What is thee doing up on deck, Nate?' it said sternly. 'Thee should be in thy bunk at this hour.'

Dido turned and saw a tall man, dressed all in black. He

17

had a long black beard almost covering his white shirt-front; his face was severe but two great mournful eyes in it seemed as if they paid little attention to the words he spoke; they were fixed elsewhere, on vacancy.

'I – I'm sorry, sir, Cap'n Casket,' Nate said, stammering a little. 'I was taking a hot drink to Uncle 'Lije when I saw the little girl had wakened up.'

'So she has. So she has. How strange,' murmured Captain Casket, bending his eyes on Dido for the first time. 'Does thee feel better for thy long sleep, my dear?'

'Yes, thank you, mister,' Dido answered bashfully.

'Nate, since the little one has woken, thee had better fetch her some slops.'

'Yes, sir, cap'n. Shall I fetch some o' Miss Du – '

'Don't be a fool, boy!' Captain Casket said sharply. 'Thee knows it is impossible. They – they would be too small. There must be some boys' gear in one of the slop chests, fetch out a bundle. And shears: that long hair won't do aboard a whaler.'

'Yes, sir.' Nate ran off in a hurry. Captain Casket fixed his sad wandering eyes on Dido but they soon moved back to the horizon and, heaving a deep sigh, he seemed to forget her. She was in too much awe of him to speak.

At length, turning to her again, he said:

'Has thee family and friends in England, my child?'

'Y-yes, sir!'

'Poor souls. This will have been a sorrowful time for them. No matter, the joy when thee is restored to them will be all the greater.'

'Yes, sir. Thank you for picking me up,' Dido said bravely.

'Providence must have ordered that we should be sailing by. His ways are strange.' Captain Casket's grave face lightened in a smile of rare sweetness and simplicity; he added, 'Now thee has wakened up, my child, thee can be of considerable help to me in thy turn.'

18

'Yes, sir. H-how?'

'Tomorrow will be soon enough to explain the task I have in mind for thee. I will not burden thee tonight. Here comes Nate now, with the clothes. When thee has put them on, thee had better sleep again.'

He moved away silently over the deck.

Nate came running with an armful of clothes and a great pair of shears. He proceeded to chop off most of Dido's hair.

'That feels better,' she said, shaking her head. 'Can't think how it come to be so long, it never used. It musta growed while I was sleeping. Why won't long hair do aboard a whaler?'

'Why? Because o' the gurry,' Nate said grinning. 'Now, can you fix yourself up in them things?'

'What's gurry?'

'Slime. You'll see at cutting-in time, if the men have had greasy luck.'

Nate had brought nankeen breeches, a shirt, a monkey-jacket, red drawers, Falmouth stockings, and a pair of leather brogans.

'These'll be too big for me,' Dido said. But she soon found they were not. 'Great snakes! I ain't half growed since I been a-laying here.'

'Guess that'll be all the whale-oil. We could see it was doin' you good. You used to cough considerable, at first, but you haven't done so for months.'

Dido looked round to make sure they were not overheard. 'What were you going to tell me about Captain Casket? And why does he talk in that queer way?'

'He's a Friend – a Quaker – that's why. And what I was going to tell you – ' Nate in his turn glanced behind him and, seeing the deck was clear, went on, 'He's allus had a kind of an uncommon fancy, you see – ever since he was a boy, Uncle 'Lije says. First-off on this trip it warn't so noticeable. His old lady, Mrs Casket, she sailed along with us because she warn't well and they reckoned sea air would do her good. But it didn't. She took sick and died, poor soul, afore we ever sighted Santa Cruz. When she was on board he kept to plain whaling. But when she died and –' Nate came to a halt and started again. 'She was a mite solemn-like and fussy in her ways, and scared to death of the sea, but there warn't no real harm in her. She used to make gingerbread and molasses cookies sometimes, afore she was took ill. Can you bake cookies?' he asked Dido.

'No.'

'Oh. Well, after she died Cap'n Casket got quieter and quieter. Never smiled – not that he was ever much of a one for a joke – never spoke. One day he said he saw the pink whale.'

'What's queer about that?' asked the ignorant Dido.

'What's queer? Well, they don't *come* pink whales, that's all! But Uncle 'Lije says Cap'n Casket for ever had this notion that one day he *would* see one. No one liked to say anything, but they thought he was a bit touched. Anyway, he swore he'd seen it and it was making north'ards and we was bound to follow it. Then Mr Slighcarp, he's the first mate, he allowed as *he'd* seen it too. Some thought he was just humouring the Old Man but anyways we chased it, up past Finisterre and Finistère and Ushant and Land's End, and next thing we was squeezing through the North Sea past London River. Clean lost the pink whale but that's where we picked *you* up. Only you was fast asleep and wouldn't wake to tell us where your home port was. For all we knew you mighta been a Fiji Islander. So I adopted you, kind of like a mascot because I'd lost my pet mynah bird. Then Cap'n Casket he sees the pink whale again, off John o' Groats, and she leads us a fair dance first south right round the Horn and then north again up past the Galapagos and Alaska to where we are now.'

'Did you ever catch her?'

'Not likely! No one's ever seed her but Mr Slighcarp and

the Old Man. Still, we had good luck, we caught plenty other whales after that first little dummy run. But some o' the men was a bit ashamed of getting so far off the whaling grounds as we was when we picked you up.'

Suddenly Dido's lip quivered.

'I wish you hadn't! I wish some English ship had picked me up!'

'Well, there's ingratitude!' Nate said indignantly. He added in a gentler tone, 'We couldn't leave you to drown, now, could we? You'll get home soon enough.'

But, for Dido, the dreamlike strangeness of her surroundings, the huge dark frosted ship, the blazing Arctic sky across which mysterious arches and curtains and streamers of red and green now flickered – most of all the fact, only half understood, that she was an immense distance, half a world away, from home – all this was suddenly too much to be borne. She flung herself down on the pile of sheepskins and cried as if her heart would break.

'There, there!' said Nate uncomfortably. 'Come now, don't take on so, don't! Supposin' somebody was to see you?'

'I don't care!' wept Dido. 'I wish I was at home. Oh, I wish I was at home *now*!'

2

The captured whale – the mysterious weeper –
Captain Casket's task

WHEN Dido woke once more dawn had broken, wild and red and dim. The ice-covered ship gleamed like a Christmas tree. What had roused her was the shouts of the men, who had returned towing a large sperm-whale; their three boats spread around it like tugs. Dido was astonished at the sight of this huge, mouse-coloured monster, almost as big as the ship, it seemed, with its steep face, flat and featureless as the side of a house. At first, in alarm, thinking it was still alive, she scrambled out of her straw bed and retreated to the far side of the deck. But then she realized that it was dead and the men were making it fast to the ship.

'What are they going to do with it?' she asked Nate, who ran along the deck with five mugs of hot coffee in each hand. By day he was revealed as a long, lanky redhead, with friendly grey eyes and a great many freckles.

'Cut-in, o' course. I can't stop now, chick. Why don't you step down to the camboose and get some breakfast? Doctor'll be astonished to see you.'

Dido guessed that the camboose must be the kitchen, but she was too interested in what the men were doing to leave the deck for a while. Several men had gone over the side and now stood on stagings like painters' cradles slung from ropes between the ship and the whale. They were armed with long-handled, sharp-edged spades. Meanwhile a huge hook, lowered from the rigging, had been sunk into the whale's side. At this point the rest of the crew all combined their strength to turn a massive windlass, while they encouraged each other by singing:

> 'Oh, whaling is my only failing,
> Sailing whaling's done for me!
> Life's all bible-leaves and bailing –
> Never ask me in when there's decent folk to tea!'

Now, to Dido's amazement, while every timber of the ship seemed to strain and strive, the body of the whale slowly began turning over in the water as the men wound the windlass-handle and pulled on the rope attached to the hook. While the whale turned, the cutters on the hanging planks skilfully sliced round its body so that the blubber, or skin, was peeled off in a spiral like orange-peel. When a considerable length of this great blubber-strip had been drawn up on the hook, sections of it as large as blankets were cut clear by the men on deck and lowered through a forward hatchway.

> 'Hush your weeping and your wailing
> Six-and-thirty months I'll be at sea,
> Tears and grumbles are unavailing –
> And never ask me in when there's decent folk to tea!'

'What do they do with it down there?' Dido asked a passing man. He scowled at her. It was Mr Slighcarp, the first mate.

'Ho! *You've* woken up to plague us, have you? Don't you go near the try-works or I'll spank you with a deck spade.'

'They mince it up, ready to be boiled down for oil,' another more good-natured man told her. 'There's a blubber-room down there, I dessay Cap'n Casket'll let you have a look some time. Mr Pardon, the second mate, will maybe show you; he's right pleased to know you've woken up at last; he's down below cutting-in now.'

> 'Keep your sturgeon, salmon, grayling,
> Shark, bonito's not for me.
> Whales are all I'll be impaling –
> And never ask me in when there's decent folk to tea!'

Dido wondered what the angry-looking Mr Slighcarp had meant by the try-works. Then she saw that an iron door had been opened at one side of the square brick structure in the middle of the deck; a fire roared inside it and men ran to and fro feeding the flames with bits of tarred rope and frizzled scraps of whale, poking the blaze with long-handled fire pikes. Two huge metal pots were built in above and into these were being tossed chunks of blubber, sliced most of the way through into paper-thin slices so that they looked like books. The brew in the try-pots began to melt and bubble: thick, black, greasy smoke rolled over the deck.

'Cor, love a lily-white *duck*!' gasped Dido, as a murky bank of the smoke surged towards her and almost smothered her. 'I never in all my born days smelt such a smell, *never*! It's enough to make a bad egg burst out crying and go home to mother.'

Nate, who was passing with the empty mugs, laughed. 'You'd better get used to it,' he said. 'There's going to be plenty more afore we're through.'

At noon a little old bow-legged Negro whom everybody addressed affectionately as Doctor came on deck with a steaming cauldron of something that smelt very appetizing, and the men helped themselves from it when they could snatch a moment from their labours.

'Go and help yourself!' Nate called to Dido – he was sharpening tools on a grindstone.

Rather timidly she approached the cook who gave her a flashing white grin and handed her a tin pannikin of hash.

'You like lobscouse, eh? Best lobscouse from here to Christmas Island, eh Mr Pardon? Make a change from whale-oil, I b'lieve?'

Mr Pardon, the white-haired, kindly-faced second mate, who was also gulping down a bowlful of food, had his mouth full and couldn't speak. But he smiled at Dido and as soon as he could, said:

'Bless me! Who'da taken you for the poor little shrivelled poke we hauled on board ten months ago? Why you're as chipper and lively as any lass in Nantucket. I reckon that ten months' rest did you a sight o' good. Eat up the lobscouse, dearie, I'll lay you can do with some solid vittles.'

'What's it made of?' Dido asked, looking suspiciously at the mixture in her pan.

'Why, corned beef and hardtack and good salt water, eat it up! You can still do wi' a bit more flesh on your bones.'

Mr Pardon hurried back to his post over the side, adjuring her as he went to 'keep clear of the gurry'.

Dido could see what he meant; by this time the whole deck was covered with an unbelievable mess of oil and slime and bits of the whale's thin outer skin. It seemed impossible that the planks should ever be clean and white again. The sails were blackened by smoke and the rigging was all furred up with greasy soot.

> 'When I'm old and weak and ailing
> Sailing whaling still I'll be;
> Lash me standing to the lash-railing –
> And never speak my name when there's decent folk to
> tea –'

came the voices from the windlass.

Dido picked up a cutting-spade and moved cautiously over the littered deck, but she had the ill-fortune to tread on a particularly slippery patch of oil, lost her footing and slid, entangling the cutting-spade between the legs of Mr Slighcarp as he stretched up to pull down a blanket of blubber from the hook. He fell sprawling with the blubber on top of him, and when he rose cursed Dido most evilly. Matters were not helped by the shouts of laughter from the crew.

'I – I'm sorry, mister,' Dido gulped. 'I couldn't help it, honest!'

'Git below!' snarled Mr Slighcarp. 'I'll have no

frog-spawn like you littering the deck while I'm in charge. Git!'

Terrified, Dido picked herself up and scurried away. Guided by a gesture and a wink from Nate, she slipped down a hatchway and found herself suddenly out of the noise and stink and bustle, on a neat little winding stair, white-painted and silent. Where did it lead? On she went, cautiously exploring, and presently entered a good-sized stateroom, also white-painted, and very tidy. A rocking-chair stood by a glowing stove; a swinging bed was made up with a patchwork quilt; over this hung a compass, upside down. Dido studied the compass for a moment but it meant nothing to her; nor did the charts spread on the table. A huge book held them down; she opened it; it was the Bible. While sniffing the petals of a blooming pink geranium on a shelf she was startled by a small sound from somewhere close at hand. It sounded like a sob.

Arrested, Dido stood motionless, listening. Yes! There again! More sobs, half stifled at first, then breaking into a low, wailing cry, *'Mamma! Oh, Mamma!'*

Dido thought she had never in her life heard a sound so lonely and desolate.

The cabin was empty; where, then, did the voice come from? There were two doors, one on each side, in the white panelling. Trying them, she found that both were locked, but the sound seemed to come from behind the right-hand one. When she tried it a frightened voice whispered, 'Who's there?'

'It's me. Dido Twite. Who are you?'

No reply. Dead silence from beyond the door. Dido tried again.

'Come on! Do say summat! I ain't a-going to bite you! Why are you shut in?'

No answer.

'Croopus,' Dido sighed to herself. 'This is a rum brig

and no mistake. Pink whales and spooky voices. Don't I jist wish I was at home with Simon!'

A whisper hit her ear like a small cold draught. She leaned to catch what it said.

'I believe you're Aunt Tribulation. *Go away!*'

'I'm Dido Twite, I tell you!'

'Go away!'

'Pooh,' said Dido, hurt. 'All right, I just will. And you can holler for me next time.' She made her way back on deck, greatly puzzled. Whose could the voice be? No one she had seen or heard of yet, that was certain. It had sounded like a child – but nobody had mentioned a child.

This time, keeping well clear of the try-works and the fierce Mr Slighcarp, she made her way to the quarterdeck. There she found Captain Casket, silent, withdrawn, and stern-looking. He had his back to her and was studying the compass in the binnacle, so she tiptoed to the rail and stood watching two gulls on an ice-floe as they quarrelled over a scrap of blubber.

Presently she felt a chilly sensation in her shoulderblades and turned to find that Captain Casket had his strange sad eyes fixed on her.

He cleared his throat once or twice, as if speaking were not a very common activity with him, and said:

'What is thy name, child?'

'D-Dido, sir. Dido Twite.'

'A heathen name,' the captain murmured. 'No matter. There may be godliness within.' He scrutinized her with an intent, close regard, as if measuring her for some purpose he had in mind. Dido looked back wonderingly.

At last he said:

'Thee has a firm chin, my child, and a philanthropic brow.'

'Has – have I?' Dido said, surprised. 'Coo, I never knew. Maybe I got some o' the gurry on it when I fell down.' She rubbed her forehead with her sleeve.

'I need thy help,' Captain Casket went on. 'Thee looks like a strong, brave character.'

Am I? Dido wondered. She realized with surprise that she did feel strong, far stronger than she had been before she fell into her ten-month sleep.

'Does thee think thee can be kind but firm with somebody not so blessed in courage and strength?'

Suddenly Dido began to guess what he was leading up to. Forgetting her slight awe of him she blurted out, 'Well, mister, if it's anything to do with that poor little thing that you got locked up downstairs I can tell you straight I think it's a wicked shame. How would *you* like to be locked up?'

Captain Casket looked at her sadly. 'Child, thee doesn't understand,' he said. 'I am not her jailer. She did it herself. She bolted herself in when her Mamma died. No words of mine avail to draw her forth.'

'Ohhhh!' Dido breathed, round-eyed. 'Mercy gracious, why ever'd she do that? Is she your little girl, then?'

'Yes,' he said, sighing.

'What's her name? How old is she?' Dido was all curiosity. What a queer thing, to shut oneself in a cabin! 'She's nine,' he said heavily. 'Her name is Dutiful Penitence Casket.'

'Croopus,' Dido murmured.

'Her Mamma, my dear wife, though endowed with every Christian virtue, had one foolish failing,' he went on, half to himself. 'This was her incurable fear of the sea. I thought that if I took her with me on a voyage it would allay her fear and improve her delicate health. Fool! Fool that I was.' He paused and added in a lower tone, 'But the ways of Providence are strange to us.'

'And so the poor lady took and died?' Dido said compassionately as he seemed to have come to a stop.

'Yes, my child. And Penitence, who had imbibed her mother's fears, believed the sea had caused her death.'

'So she shut herself up.'

'From that day to this,' he agreed, sighing. 'I believe she thinks the sea will kill her too, if she ventures out.'

'Coo,' said Dido. 'What a jobberknoll. But what does she do for prog – for vittles?'

'The little cabin where she slept next to my wife is also the store where my dear Sarah kept preserves and spices and medicines. I believe Penitence has been living on beach-plum jelly and sassefras all this time.'

'What a do, eh? Don't she never *wash*?' said Dido with the liveliest interest.

'There is a little hatch through which I can sometimes get a glimpse of her and through which a basin of water may be passed.'

'Well, my Ma would soon clobber me if I went on in such a way,' said Dido frankly. 'And if you was to ask me, *I* think she sounds touched in the upper works. But I can see what you wants. You wants me to put the wheedle on her and make her come out, ain't that so?'

'Yes, my child. Thee has guessed right. I have a hatred of violence or trickery; I would not force her to come out. But if thee can somehow *persuade* her . . .'

He looked at Dido hopefully, and added: 'After all, we did pull thee out of the sea. We saved thy life.'

'Yes,' muttered Dido ungratefully, 'and if you hadn't I might a bin picked up by an English ship and safe home now, instead o' freezing at the fishy back end o' nowhere. Anyways, why didn't you ask Nate or Mr Pardon to have a go with the little girl?'

Captain Casket appeared slightly embarrassed. At last he said, 'My child, I tell thee this in confidence. The crew are not aware that Penitence has locked herself up in this way. They – they believe that she is ailing. To have it known that she defies me would be bad for discipline. Thee –' he gazed at her anxiously – 'thee will not divulge what I have told thee, my dear?'

'Oh, *now* I twig your lay,' Dido said. He looked bewildered. 'I see why you been so havey-cavey about her. All right, I'll keep mum. And I don't mind having a try.'

'Thee is a good child. I am truly grateful,' Captain Casket said almost humbly. 'I feel thee may succeed where I have failed.'

Dido gave him a sharp look. 'Ain't trying to butter me up, are you? If I manage to wheedle her out in the fresh air, so you ain't shamed when we gets to port and she won't come out, will you see I gets a passage on the fust ship that'll take me back to England?'

'Anything in my power I shall do,' he assured her quickly. 'As soon as we return to New Bedford I shall inquire about sailings.'

'What'll happen to Dutiful Penitence – glad *I* wasn't saddled with such a handle – then?'

'Oh, my sister Tribulation will look after her,' Captain Casket said, avoiding her eyes. 'Now I must leave thee to oversee the cutting-in. Good-bye, my child. Thee may have the use of my stateroom. I will move into Mr Slighcarp's cabin.'

As he walked aft, rather fast, Dido stared after him thoughtfully. Why had he been so anxious to get away? Somehow she felt that, although he seemed a good man, she could not entirely trust Captain Casket. He had more in his mind than he had told her. And she thought poorly of him for allowing his daughter to get the upper hand in so decided a way. Weak, she thought. He means well but he's weak. That's the sort that allus lets you down in the end.

Still, she thought, I can look after meself. I'm a big girl now, near as big as Simon. And she surveyed her extra six inches with pride before squatting down, chin on fists, to consider the problem of how Dutiful Penitence Casket was to be persuaded out of her shell.

3

Talking to Penitence – the veiled lady – hopscotch –
Dido makes a promise

LONG after dark had fallen Dido was still squatting on the
quarter-deck, her brow wrinkled in thought. Twice since
her talk with Captain Casket she had gone below, tapped on
the panel in the captain's stateroom and tried to persuade
the hidden occupant of the little room beyond to come out.
Her first attempt had met with no response; next time the
only reaction had been a fierce, miserable whisper from
behind the panel:

'Go away. Go *away*! Whoever you are I shan't come out.
I know you're only trying to trick me to go up on deck and
be drowned!'

Dido saw that she would have to be clever.

'What do you do all day long in there?' she asked, the
beginnings of a plan sprouting in her mind. There was no
answer. She had not really expected one. She went on, half
to herself: 'Well, I don't wonder you gets blue-devilled if
you does nothing but sit and think o' drowning all the
time. Cheesy, *I* calls it!'

She left the cabin, shutting the door behind her with a
loud annoying slam.

After more than sixteen hours of frantic, continuous
work the captured whale had been all cut up and melted
down; Mr Slighcarp's watch staggered below, blind and
speechless with fatigue. At last the moment arrived that
Dido had been waiting for. She stretched, rose, left the
quarter-deck, and went along to the try-works, which
were simmering down, now, to a dull red glow. Half-a-
dozen weary men were scrubbing the deck with ashes;

their shadows flitted to and fro under a towering Arctic moon. From time to time they paused in their labours, dipped bits of hardtack in the still molten blubber and chewed them. The good-natured Mr Pardon was supervising the work.

'Why, dearie,' he said in surprise, 'you shoulda been in your bunk hours agone. Cap'n Casket tells me he's given you his stateroom for to be company for little Miss Penitence. Mr Slighcarp's not best pleased at having to move in with me, but 'tis more fitting for you than lying here on a donkey's breakfast. And I guess you'll be better able than a man to look after that poor little ailing lass.'

Dido nodded soberly. 'Mr Pardon,' she said.

'Well, dearie?'

'What's Captain Casket's little girl like?'

'Like?' Mr Pardon scratched his white head, puzzled. 'Why, I guess she's like all little gals. Sews her sampler, reads her lesson – Mrs Casket allus used to hear her lessons when she was alive, poor lady.'

'But what's she like?' Dido persisted. 'What kind o' games does she like to play?'

'Play? Why, I dunno as how she plays any *games*. But my nephew Nate here'd know better'n I do; his home's not too far from the Casket place.'

'Games?' said Nate when appealed to. 'Don't reckon she ever played any. Very quiet little thing, sorta peaky. Her ma allus kept her pretty much at her stitching and so forth.'

'Blimey,' muttered Dido, 'what a set-out. No wonder she's such a misery. Mr Pardon, d'you reckon as how you could make me a shuttlecock for her? Out o' whalebone or summat? I could stick it with gulls' feathers.'

'I don't see why not,' Mr Pardon said doubtfully. 'Guess it would be simple enough. But what would Cap'n Casket think? Mrs Casket allus used to say that toys were inventions of the Devil.'

'I guess he'd have to put up with it,' Dido said. 'He asked me if I'd try to take Dutiful Penitence outa herself. She's pining for her ma.'

Nate was interested in the scheme. 'I could make a whalebone bat,' he offered. 'And some checkers or spillikins.'

'Could you? That'd be bang-up!'

Dido went below, well pleased with the way matters were shaping.

The big cabin was lit up by a hanging whale-oil lamp. Dido turned the wick up to its brightest. Then she listened. No sound came from Dutiful Penitence, so Dido banged the cabin door, opened and shut some drawers several times as loudly as she could, and overturned a chair with a tremendous clatter.

She heard a sleepy stir from beyond the panel. 'Papa, what's the matter?' said a scared voice. 'Is it a storm?'

Dido made no answer. She climbed up on to the chart table and then, after carefully judging the distance, jumped four feet to a wall shelf, where she clung like a squirrel. From there, making use of the hanging compass, she swung to the bed, landing with a thud. Then she crawled to the bed-foot, put her knee on an open drawer, and clawed herself across to another shelf, aware, as she did so, though without showing it, that the panel had opened a crack and that she was being watched. She balanced on the shelf, gauging the distance to a chair.

'Who are you?' asked an astonished voice. 'And what *do* you think you're doing? Where is Papa?'

'I told you already,' Dido said without looking round. 'I'm Dido Twite. Your pa's given me his cabin.' She steadied herself and sprang. The chair fell, and threw her to the ground. 'Drat it,' Dido said coldly, getting up and rubbing her knee. 'Now I shall have to start again.'

'Start *what* again?'

Taking no notice of the question, Dido climbed back on

to the chart table. This time she chose a different route, throwing herself like a flying-fox on to a large sea-chest, which seemed full of bottles, to judge from the loud clatter when she landed on it.

She scowled in concentration, considering a sideways clamber across the door as against an awkward diagonal jump to the bed. She chose the former.

'What are you doing?' the voice repeated.

Dido dragged herself up with difficulty and turned round. She was now perching like a gargoyle on a sort of dresser. 'Why!' she said exasperatedly. 'What d'you think I'm doing? What does it *look* as if I'm doing? Making cheese? I'm getting round the room without touching the floor, o' course. I shoulda thought any ninny coulda seen *that*. You must be a slow-top. Now, don't interrupt again, you put me off.' She knit her brows and pressed her lips together, then with a mighty spring succeeded in launching herself from the dresser to the fallen chair, which slid conveniently across to the bed.

'Now I'm going to sleep,' Dido announced. 'Mind you don't make a noise and wake me.' She turned out the light. All this time she had never looked towards the open hatchway. Yawning loudly she snuggled down under the blankets. Silence fell.

After a longish pause the voice asked:

'Why didn't you want to touch the floor?'

Dido made no answer, but, instead, let out a slight snore.

Very early next morning Dido, who needed little sleep after her ten-month nap, woke and scurried up on deck before any sound came from Dutiful Penitence.

The *Sarah Casket*, all her barrels now filled with whale-oil, was speeding south under a clear sky. Already the icy mountains of Alaska were out of sight. Some of the men were hard at work hammering in the lids of the great hogsheads, twice the height of Dido, before these were lowered into the hold; others were scrubbing every inch of the deck and bulwarks with ashes and bits of blubber, even climbing into the rigging to wipe the shrouds. Soot and ashes flew away on the fresh breeze, and the ship by degrees began to look so tidy and clean that Dido could hardly believe it was the same in which, only the day before, whale-oil had run like greasy dark ink over the deck.

The kindly Mr Pardon had contrived time out of his duties to make a shuttlecock. He gave it to Dido. 'It ain't very grand; I made a bit of a mux of it,' he apologized. 'But I reckoned you'd ruther have it *soon* than *fancy*. I'll make a better one now I got the hang – I'm real pleased to do it. Young 'uns should have playthings. And Nate, he's fixing ye a right handsome battledore but 'twon't be finished yet a piece because Mr Slighcarp's sent him up to scrub the crow's nest.'

Dido looked up and saw a tiny figure, miles up it seemed in the clear piercing air. Nate waved a scrubbing-brush cheerfully and she waved back.

'This here's a fust-rate shuttlecock,' she told Mr Pardon. 'Just what I wanted. Cap'n Casket's little girl will be astonished, I reckon.'

'Don't forget your breakfast, dearie,' Mr Pardon said as she turned to go below.

'That's a notion,' Dido said. She added to herself: 'I dessay Dutiful Pen has had enough o' plum jelly to last a lifetime; let's see what a sight o' summat else does for her.' She skipped along to the camboose by the wheelhouse. 'What's for breakfast?' she asked briskly.

'Ah! Is little chick passenger!' The black cook gave her his beaming grin. 'I have nice fu-fu, also nice plum duff.'

'Can I have two helps o' plum duff? I'll take some down for Dutiful P. She might fancy it.'

'Is picky and choosy, that one,' the cook said, shaking his head. 'Is not fancy my cooking.' However, he dealt out two large portions of delicious raisin pudding, made with dripping and potash.

'You like some coffee?'

'Thanks, mister. Any milk?'

'Not yet, honey. Goat she took and died. In some month we make Galapagos Island. Then maybe coconut milk.'

Dido ran down the companionway with the food and sat down at the chart table, where she began to eat one portion of plum duff with smacking sounds of enjoyment.

'Nibblish good prog,' she remarked loudly. 'Better'n my ma makes, anyhow.'

When she had finished her plateful she got up, leaving the second portion untouched and well in view, took the shuttlecock out of her pocket, and began to kick it into the air. As Mr Pardon had said, it was not a very well-made one, being slightly unbalanced, and at first Dido found difficulty in keeping it up for more than two or three kicks. She persevered, however, bounding about the room until she was breathless and bruised from collisions with the furniture. She noticed that the panel had opened an inch and an eye was peering at her with silent, astonished attention.

'This room ain't big enough,' Dido complained presently, when she was becoming more experienced with the shuttlecock and had worked her score up to twenty-three. 'I'm a-going on deck, I am, where there's plenty of room.'

She departed, slamming the door behind her. Although strongly tempted to linger and look through the keyhole, she knew this would be foolish. Instead she clattered up the companion stair and went out to the quarter-deck.

However she soon found that there was little room, even here, to practise her game, for the men were tidying out the hold, to make room for the last casks of whale-oil, and had brought all the stores up on deck: bundles of hoops and staves, great sides of salt beef, sacks of hardtack, and a whole mass of other gear lay heaped in disorder. The casks

37

of oil in the hold were being hosed, to keep them water-tight, and there was such a general hubbub of to-and-fro activity that Dido seemed to be constantly underfoot and in everybody's way. Nate, playing on a sort of zither made of whalebone, helped the men keep time.

They were singing:

'Strong to Pleasant, Wake to Guam
    Winds are favouring, seas are calm,
Midway down to Pokaaku
    Typhoon cuts our mainmast through.

'Easter, Disappointment, Nome,
    Through the watery world we roam,
Tristan, Fogo, Trinidad,
    Winds contrary, weather bad,
Christmas, Easter, Kwajalein –
    When shall we see Brant Point again?'

The zither gave Dido an idea. There were bundles of whalebone pieces lying about the deck, of assorted sizes and shapes. 'I reckon they can spare me a bit,' she said to herself. 'I won't bother to ask Cap'n Casket, he looks a mite cagged.'

The captain was taking no part in the bustle; he leaned against the mainmast with his eyes fixed on the far horizon.

Dido picked up a piece of bone about the size of a walking-stick and quietly made off with it.

'Now all I want's a tool; land's sakes, they must have plenty on a ship this size if I could find out where they keeps 'em.'

There was a smith's forge by the foremast and a carpenter's bench aft of the try-works but both these were too much under observation at present; hoping to find other stores Dido nipped down the forward hatchway into the blubber-room. This was unoccupied, now, and silent; a sort of tide-mark on the wall showed where yesterday the blubber had been stacked kneedeep. At the moment the

38

room was being used for the temporary storage of things taken from the hold; a pile of oakum and sail-canvas occupied most of the floor. Dido turned to leave, seeing nothing she could use, but then stopped, arrested by the unexpected sight of a boot protruding from under the canvas.

It was bottle-green, elastic sided, quite unlike the brogans worn by the sailors. It looked like an English lady's boot. Where could it have come from? Puzzled and inquisitive, Dido gave it a tug, and then jumped back with a yelp of alarm as the boot disappeared swiftly beneath the canvas. There was a foot inside it!

Curiosity overcoming her caution, Dido approached the heap once more and pulled aside some folds of canvas. A sort of writhing motion went on in the middle of the heap, the sailcloth was displaced, and suddenly, rather as a serpent darts out of its lair, the figure of a tall, veiled lady uncoiled and shot out from under the pile of stuff. She towered over the quailing Dido, who would have run for it had she not been held fast by the ear.

'What do you think you are doing here?' the lady said in a low, grating tone.

'P-p-please, ma'am, I d-didn't mean no harm!' gulped Dido. 'I was only looking for a c-c-corkscrew!'

'A likely story! Prying and meddling where you'd no business to be! Repulsive child! You deserve to be severely punished. Now, listen here, miss!'

'Y-y-yes, ma'am?'

'If you so much as mention that you have seen me to anyone – anyone at all – I shall learn of it. And it will be the worse for you. You wish to return to England, do you not?'

'Yes, ma'am,' Dido whispered, very much astonished.

'Then you had better keep a still tongue in your head! Otherwise your chances of ever seeing London River again are very, very small. Do you understand? Now – *go*!'

Dido needed no encouragement – something in the veiled lady's aspect had struck her with mortal terror – but she received a final warning in the form of a box on the ear, that shot her out of the doorway.

Numb and chattering with fright she scurried up the companionway and back on deck. Luckily nobody had noticed her come out. The whole crew were trying to manhandle a spare anchor out of its usual resting-place so as to cram a few casks of oil underneath it. Frightened though she was, Dido kept her wits about her; she grabbed a handful of tools from the carpenter's bench and then, still gasping for breath, ran down to the captain's cabin.

She was too discomposed to notice that the hatchway shut with a click as she entered the room, but she did observe, when a little more recovered, that the plum duff on the second plate had been eaten. She grinned to herself and, sitting up, inspected the tools she had taken. Choosing a drill, she set to work on her whalebone rod.

It proved a long, fiddling task, which occupied most of the day. Though aware that she was often watched, Dido pretended not to notice. She found it impossible to work all the time, for her fingers became stiff. Twice she broke off to make a tour of the room without touching the deck, each time attempting a new route. She also played several games of shuttlecock, and chalked herself out a hopscotch square on the chart table. Here she encountered a difficulty, however.

'I wisht as how I had a pebble,' she remarked aloud. 'Or a marble, or a penny, or even a button would do. Oh well,' heaving a deep sigh, 'can't play hopscotch, that's all. Funny how I has a *fancy* to play hopscotch. Anyway I reckon it's dinner-time; I'll nip up to the camboose and see what's cooking.'

She took the empty plates and left the room.

All the time she had been working and playing part of her mind was occupied with the puzzle of the mysterious veiled lady in the blubber-room. Could she be a stowaway? Dido wondered. She might have been hidden in the hold and obliged to take refuge elsewhere because of the general turnout. But where could she have come on board? What did she live on? Did none of the crew know about her presence?

'Somebody must know,' Dido said to herself as she absently accepted two bowls of porpoise chowder from the cook, '*somebody* must know, and musta told her about me. Else how did she twig I was English? I wonder who told her?'

She returned to the cabin, ate her meal, and flung herself on the bed for a nap, burying her face in the pillow and letting out snores. For a long time there was silence; then she heard a cautious clink. She redoubled her snores, shutting her eyes so tightly that she saw red and green stars. Presently the hatch was heard to close with a gentle click. For good measure Dido lay five minutes longer, then, yawning loudly, she opened her eyes. The second chowder bowl was empty. Beside it lay a larger leather button.

'Well I never!' Dido exclaimed in astonishment. 'Fancy my not noticing that there button afore! Jist what I needed for hopscotch! Now, can I remember the rules, I wonder?'

Having dumped the chowder bowls on the floor she climbed on to the table. Addressing herself as if she were a slow-witted pupil she proceeded to rehearse the rules of hopscotch. She was thus occupied when the door opened unexpectedly and she met Captain Casket's startled eyes.

'Is – is thee all right, my child?' he asked.

'Now look here,' said Dido crossly. 'Let's get this straight from the fust. You gives me your cabin, right, then it's *mine*. See? I don't expect no monnicking and chissicking – no *interference*,' she explained impatiently as she met his questioning gaze. 'You keep outa here. Ain't you got the ship to look arter? You go watch for that pink whale o' yourn. *I'll* tell you if you're wanted here.'

She gave him such a fierce scowl that he retreated, gingerly shutting the door. 'That's got rid o' *him*,' Dido said with satisfaction. 'Now maybe we can tend to business.'

She practised hopscotch very enjoyably for an hour or so, then worked on her piece of whalebone. When this was completely hollowed out into a tube she made a mouthpiece at one end and a series of holes along it. If blown on hard enough it produced a plaintive sound, like the call of a hungry bird. After much labour Dido had several notes adjusted to her satisfaction, and was able to play 'God Save King Jim' and 'Who'll Buy My Sweet Lavender?' This was received with awestruck and flattering silence from the watcher behind the panel.

'I wisht I knowed a few more tunes,' Dido said at length. 'Seems as how while I'd been asleep I forgot most o' the ones I used to know. Ah well – maybe I'll remember some more tomorrow. I'll jist step out for a breath o' fresh air now, and then go to kip.'

She went in search of Nate, and found him sprawled on the main deck, weaving a rope mat in a rather inattentive and dreamy fashion while he tried over the words of a chanty.

'Oh it's gally and roll, me boys, ripple and run,
So hold to your hand-lance, the chase has begun,
Tally-ho! till she breaches, come, join in the fun
    We're off on a Nantucket sleigh-ride.

'It's flurry and scurry, she bolts and she sounds
And something and something tum tiddle tum grounds
And something else ending in bounds or in rounds
    Hey ho! for a Nantucket sleigh-ride.

'Oh, hallo, chick,' he broke off, on seeing Dido. 'I've got summat for you. Finished it as soon as old man Slighcarp went below.' And he brought out a beautiful little battledore, ingeniously made from woven strips of bone.

'Coo!' said Dido. 'It's naffy! Ain't you clever? I'll lay Dutiful Pen won't be able to hold off when she sees this! Could you make another one, d'you reckon?'

'Guess so,' Nate said agreeably. He started singing again:

> 'Tum tiddle tum tiddle tum tiddle tum grounds
> Pull on! head to head as his noddle he rounds . . .

'Can you think of a rhyme for sounds, chick?'

Dido could not. 'Does you make 'em up, then?' she asked, much impressed.

'Sure.'

Finding Nate such a kindred spirit Dido showed him her whalebone pipe.

'That's cunning,' he said, blowing on it. 'Mighty smart work for a liddle 'un. Who learned you to do that?'

'My pa,' Dido said proudly. 'He plays on the hoboy, so he learned me how to make a tootlepipe.'

'Say, we'll be able to have some fine concerts now when old Slighcarp's under hatches.'

'It's time I was under hatches too,' Dido remarked, looking up at the moon. ''Night, Nate.' And she added to herself, 'I've a kind of a notion that Dutiful P might surface tonight, so I'd best be there.'

It had been an energetic day, with the hopscotch, the shuttlecock, the climbing, and hard work on the pipe; Dido turned out the lamp as soon as she reached the cabin, flung herself on the bed, and went straight to sleep.

About two hours later she found herself suddenly broad awake. The *Sarah Casket* was still speeding south before a following wind; Dido could feel the rush of the great seas as they lifted and drove past the ship's side. Every timber creaked, and even down here the hum of wind in the rigging could be heard. Moonlight came through the ports; a patch of it on the floor hardly shifted, so steady was the ship on her course.

Dido wondered what had woken her.

Then she felt the clutch of little cold hands on her arm.

'Who is it?' she whispered.

'It's me. Dutiful Penitence.'

'Ain't you cold, jist? Best come under the quilt, hadn't you?' Dido said matter-of-factly. She felt a small shape huddle up against her under the patchwork. Just at this moment the steersman evidently altered course a point or so, and the oblong of moonshine slid round, revealing the visitor.

She was a thin little creature, frail-looking as a cobweb (and no wonder, if she's been living on plum jelly ever since Santa Cruz, thought Dido), with long silvery hair, not very well brushed. She stared gravely at Dido.

'Are you really a girl?' she asked after a while.

'Yes, what d'you think? A mermaid?'

'But where did you come from?'

'Your pa picked me up, off the coast of England. I was in a ship what caught fire and sank. And I've been asleep for ten months – so Nate says – all the time you was in storage.'

'You were *in the sea*? Didn't you get scared?'

'It wasn't bad. I hung on to a spar.'

'You must be brave! Are you English?'

'Yus. And don't I jist wish I was back in England,' Dido remarked with feeling. 'But your pa says he'll put me on a boat from New Bedford, wherever that is.'

'Near Nantucket. We may unload there before going home. But I don't suppose I *shall* be going home now,' Dutiful Penitence said drearily. 'There'd be nobody to look after me except Aunt Tribulation, Papa says, and I won't stay with *her*. Maybe Cousin Ann Allerton will have me in New Bedford.'

'Who's Aunt Tribulation?' Dido asked. She had heard the name before. Could this be the lady in the blubber-room?

'Papa's sister. She's dreadfully sharp and unkind. She

lives in Vine Rapids now but she came to stay once and up-set me and Mamma. Oh, she did upset us! She told dear Mamma that she was a fool, bringing me up to be a cry-baby. Papa wanted to leave me with her when he took Mamma to sea, but I heard Mamma say she wouldn't dream of allowing it; she said Aunt Tribulation was a real dragon, and it was lucky she'd no children of her own, for her rough, slapdash ways would probably be the death of any child she had charge of. Mamma wouldn't want me to stay with a dragon.'

'What does she look like?'

'I can't remember – quite. I was only five when she came. I remember her scolding me, and saying I was a little wet-goose, because I was afraid of her dog.'

'Hum,' said Dido. 'For a sea-captain's daughter you certainly are a rum 'un, Dutiful. And, look here, whoever tied that handle to you musta been dicked in the nob and *I'm* not going to lay my tongue round it every time. I'll call you Pen. Agreeable?'

'Yes, thank you,' Penitence said shyly. 'No one ever gave me a short name before. How old are you, Dido?'

'I've sorta lost count,' Dido admitted. 'With the long nap and all. Round about eleven, I reckon. What did you do all the time shut in that cupboard, Pen?'

'Oh, it wasn't bad. Come and see.'

They lit the lamp and Penitence showed Dido her little room. It was really a store-cupboard with shelves all round, but one of them had been turned into a bunk. There were a few lesson-books, writing materials, sewing-things, and rows and rows of empty jelly bottles.

'I did lots of lessons,' Penitence explained, 'and I read the Bible and learned a hymn every day. Shall I say one?'

'Not jist now, thanks,' Dido answered promptly. 'Croo-pus, ain't you *good*, though? Didn't you never get fed up?'

'Oh no. I kept a journal – but it wasn't very interesting,'

Penitence confessed. 'And I worked on my sampler.' She held up an extremely large square, embroidered in cross-stitch with a ship and whales and gulls and a long piece of poetry beginning, 'Myfterious Magnet! Ere thy ufe was known, Fear clad the Deep in horrors not its own.' It was nearly finished.

'I'd sooner have done roses and doves,' Penitence went on, 'but dear M-Mamma thought it would please Papa if it had sea things. I began it when I was six.'

'Well!' said Dido. 'I'd ha' been blue-devilled in here. Specially when it's such prime fun on deck.'

Penitence shivered. 'I couldn't *bear* to go on deck. That dreadful sea! I know I'd fall in! And all the cross, rough men, and the horrid smells and dirt. Mamma always said it was dangerous up there. You won't try to make me go, will you?'

'Bless you, no. It ain't my affair. Anyhows we can have a bang-up time in the cabin now you've decided to come out and be civil.'

'Will you teach me that game with the feathered thing? And play tunes on your pipe?'

'Course I will. Us'll have rare fun.'

'You don't think Mamma would mind?' Penitence said hesitantly. 'She said playing games was a sin.'

'*Croo* –' Dido began, but bit the words back.

Her own parents, as she recalled, had never seemed particularly kind or fond of her, but at least they were quite *sensible*; all that was said of Mrs Casket, however, seemed to suggest that the woman had been an utter fool. Musta been queer in her attic, Dido thought. 'Reckon she knows better now?' she suggested gruffly. 'Lawks, if you never played, what *did* you do at home?'

'Helped with the housework.'

'Well I done that too. But I played arterwards.'

'After I'd done my tasks Mamma used to let me sit on her lap while she read the Bible,' said Penitence. Her composure faltered. 'If – if I'd been extra good, she used – she used to sing a h-hymn – '

Here, breaking down altogether, Penitence threw herself on the bed, buried her head in the quilt and cried. She cried very much indeed.

Dido looked at her worriedly. There was little consolation to offer. Foolish, Mrs Casket may have been, but her daughter had plainly thought the world of her.

'Don't take on so,' Dido said after a while, with awkward sympathy. 'Want a hankersniff? I've got one.'

But as Penitence made no reply, just went on crying and shivering and choking, Dido sat down on the floor by her, feeling oddly grown-up and capable and protective, and put an arm round her.

'Cheer up,' she muttered. 'I'll keep an eye on you. It won't work out so bad. You'll see.'

The small silvery head rubbed against her.

'Will you? Will you really?'

'That I will.'

'And when we get home to Nantucket? Will you stay with me then? So's Papa don't leave me all alone with Aunt Tribulation? I'd die if I was to be looked after by a dragon. Please? *Please!*'

The thin arms came round Dido's neck in a tight hug, so that she could hardly breathe.

'Well – maybe,' Dido said reluctantly. 'Just for a little while. You know, I dessay your Aunt Trib ain't so dragonish really. But till your pa gets you fixed up with somebody else – '

'Oh, you are kind! You're so much braver than I am. I'm scared of *everything*. But you've even been in the *sea*! If you'll – if you'll stay with me it will be much better. Will you promise?'

'All right,' Dido said, sighing.

'Would you – would you sing something now? That song you were singing before?'

'All right,' said Dido again. She began to sing in a small gruff voice:

> 'Who'll buy my sweet lavender?
> Three bunches a penny!
> Fresh picked in Sevenoaks this morning,
> Three bunches a penny!'

She stroked the tousled head. It lay heavily on her shoulder, and before long drooped in sleep.

Dido sat and stared at the lamp, which they had forgotten to turn out. Presently its yellow flame swelled and wavered in a blur of tears. Resolutely she blinked them away. It was stupid to be homesick when she knew her family wouldn't be missing her much anyway, if at all.

4

*Encouraging Pen – the Galapagos – gamming with the Martha –
Mr Slighcarp's strange behaviour –
round the Horn and back to New Bedford*

'Psst! Hey! Cap'n – Cap'n Casket! Will you step this-away?'

Captain Casket started, as Dido's voice roused him from his usual sad reverie; he turned and saw her standing behind him.

Making sure that no one could overhear she came close to him and hissed conspiratorially:

'I've done it! She's out!'

Captain Casket appeared thunderstruck.

'On deck?'

'No, no, no, gaffer. Not yet. Give us time. But she's out in the cabin eatin' of plum duff and a-playin' hopscotch. I'll have her on the deck one o' these days, though, s'long as you don't come creating and badgering.'

'Thee is a remarkable child,' Captain Casket said solemnly.

'I say though,' Dido went on, 'what 'bout this Auntie Trib, then? She fair gives young Pen the horrors. Pen thinks she's a dragon. It'll be all my work for Habakkuk if Pen finds Auntie Trib's going to have charge of her in Nantucket; she'll snib herself up in the pantry again before you can say whale-o!'

Captain Casket looked harassed. 'Sister Tribulation is really a most estimable character,' he murmured. 'She is endowed with every Christian virtue.'

'You allus says that,' Dido interjected.

'My poor Sarah – my poor wife never understood her.

But I am sure that *thee* could persuade Dutiful Penitence to like her aunt, my child.'

'That's as maybe,' Dido said dryly. 'Anyhows, you better consider if there ain't somebody else as could do the job. I'm a-warning you, see? Blimey, on an island the size of Nantucket' – Dido had found it on the map by now – 'there must be somebody else as would have charge of her. Now, I'm a-going to teach Dutiful P to play shuttlecock; lor, I don't wonder the poor little tyke's so mopish. She ain't had no upbringing at all!'

It took several weeks of Dido's company and encouragement before Penitence could be persuaded on deck. Dido was too shrewd to hurry her. They played endless games in the cabin, sang songs, asked riddles, and talked, each telling the other the whole story of her life. Penitence was quite amazed by Dido's tales of the London streets and could never hear enough about the fairs and the fights, the street markets, Punch and Judy shows, glimpses of grand people in their carriages, and the little Scottish King James III, against whom the Hanoverians were always plotting.

'Fancy living in such a great city!' Penitence said dreamily. 'Why, where we lived in Nantucket it's almost five miles to the next *house*.'

'Wouldn't suit me,' Dido said. 'I likes a bit o' life and company.'

'My mamma didn't like it either. She came from Boston. When Papa went to sea,' Pen confessed, 'she used to take me for long visits to Cousin Ann in New Bedford. We didn't stay in Nantucket much.'

Dido had become quite fond of Pen by now – there was more in the funny little thing than met the eye – but none the less it was a relief to run up on deck now and then, to talk to Nate and joke with the sailors; after a few hours of Pen's company she felt she wanted to shout and jump and climb into the rigging. Pen had grown absolutely devoted to her and, Dido considered, was coming out of her mopey ways very well.

Pen still kept her quiet tastes, though; she liked to spend several hours a day doing lessons and sewing; she offered to read the Bible or hymns to Dido but this, for the most part, Dido politely refused.

'Tell you what, though,' she suggested. 'How 'bout asking your pa if we can invite Nate to come down and sing you some o' his songs? He knows a rare lot, and on top o' that he's allus rattling off new ones. Wouldn't you like it, eh?'

Penitence looked doubtful. 'Is he very big? He isn't rough? He wouldn't tease me or hurt me?'

'Now, *Pen*! Don't you know me better'n that by now? Would I ask him if he was liable to do such blame-fool things? I'm *surprised* at you!'

Pen apologized, Captain Casket's permission was obtained, and Nate, rather bashfully, came down to the stateroom with his zither. At first Penitence trembled a good deal at the close presence of such a tall, lanky, red-headed creature, and was quite speechless with shyness. But when Nate sang:

'Oh, fierce is the Ocean and wild is the Sound
But the isle of Nantucket is where I am bound,
Sweet isle of Nantucket! where the grapes are so red,
And the light flashes nightly on Sankaty Head!'*

she was quite delighted, clapped her hands, and exclaimed, 'Oh that *is* pretty! Sing it again!'

Nate sang it again, and many others. Dido, curled up under the chart table, hugged her knees and congratulated herself. From that day, Nate was a welcome visitor in the cabin: in fact he was with them singing a song about the high-rolling breakers on the south shore of Nantucket, and

* Actually Sankaty Light was not built till 1850, but for the purpose of this book I have brought it into existence thirty years earlier.

the brave fishermen who launched their dories through the foam, when a sudden shout from the deck startled them.

'Land! Land-ho!'

'Must have sighted the Galapagos!' said Nate, scrambling to his feet. 'Blame it, why wasn't I up aloft? Cap'n Casket allus gives half a dollar to the first one that sights land. See you later, gals!' And he bolted out.

'How about it, Pen?' Dido said carelessly. 'Coming up for a look-see? Nate says there are giant tortoises on the Galapagos, as big as tea tables.'

Pen hesitated, in an agony of indecision; at last she agreed.

Dido was quite glad of the chance to bring Pen on deck when Mr Slighcarp would be ashore, buying fresh fruit and vegetables; the rest of the men were kind and friendly to her but the first mate always had a scowl and a harsh word; she had been rather anxious about the effect of this on Penitence. Luckily the deck was quite empty when, clutching Dido's hand in a tight grip, Penitence timidly followed her up the companionway and came blinking into the sunshine.

'Oh,' she breathed in astonishment. 'Isn't it *bright*? And warm! I thought we were in the Arctic.'

'We left that behind weeks ago,' Dido said kindly. 'Sit down on a coil o' rope, you're all of a tremble.'

Penitence sank down obediently. In the bright sunshine her face seemed as pale as a primrose, and contrasted strangely with Dido's healthy tan. At first she was pitiably nervous; her great blue eyes widened and she clasped Dido's hand violently whenever a wavecrest broke near the ship.

Unfortunately the land was too far away for much to be visible except a low-lying mass with some scrubby trees on it. But they were excited to see another ship, the *Martha*, anchored not far off.

Presently Captain Casket wandered along towards them.

He started uncontrollably when he saw Penitence, but Dido gave him such a fierce scowl of warning that he tried to conceal his astonishment and only said:

'I am glad to see thee out in the fresh air at last, Daughter. Thee must get some roses into thy cheeks like those of thy little friend.'

Penitence made an awkward bob, and answered, 'Yes, Papa,' in such a subdued tone that it was hardly audible; she seemed greatly relieved when he walked away along the deck.

Soon there came a hail from the *Martha*, and a boat was lowered and rowed towards them; a cheerful red-faced man called: 'Jabez! Cap'n Jabez Casket! Are you there? Can I come aboard for a gam? I've some mail for you, only eight months out o' New Bedford.'

'Come aboard and welcome, Cap'n Bilger,' Captain Casket called, and the skipper of the *Martha* was swung aboard. He handed over a batch of letters for the *Sarah Casket*'s captain and crew, and asked if they could spare any ship's biscuits as most of his had been spoiled by a leak; he offered coffee and Lemon Syrup in exchange (which the cook was glad to accept since Pen had eaten all the jelly).

'Concern it!' exclaimed Captain Bilger, slapping his leg in annoyance. 'If I haven't forgotten to bring over that blame bird!'

'Bird? What bird?' Captain Casket inquired.

'Why, a bird belonging to that boy of yours, Nate Pardon. One of my men caught it flapping about the streets of New Bedford before we sailed and recognized it as his; we've had it aboard ever since. I'll be thankful to see the last of it, I can tell you. That bird would talk the ears off a brass monkey. Now I come to think, I've another letter for you, as well. It got a mite damp, came unstuck, and I put it aside from the others. My memory's fuller of holes'n a dip-net.'

'No matter,' said Captain Casket. 'My men can call

round by the *Martha* when they come back from provisioning and pick up the bird and the letter. Young Nate will be glad to see his pet.'

The two captains went below to gossip and, an early tropical dusk falling soon after, Dido and Penitence also retired to their cabin to play hunt the thimble and speculate as to what sort of things Nate's bird would be able to say.

Pen was quite tired out by the fresh air and the excitement of being on deck; she soon went to bed and to sleep. Dido, however, was not sleepy; she returned to lean on the rail and gaze wistfully at the lights on shore. Presently she heard Captain Bilger taking his leave, and later still the men returned. Having been instructed by signals with a lantern they rowed round by the *Martha* and picked up Nate's bird, but Dido heard Mr Slighcarp telling Captain Casket that Captain Bilger found he had been mistaken about the extra letter; it was after all not for him but for the captain of some other ship.

Nate was overjoyed to recover his bird, which he had never expected to see again, and showed it off proudly to Dido.

'His name's Mr Jenkins. Ain't he beautiful?'

Dido admired the bird's glossy black plumage and brilliant yellow bill.

'What does he say?'

The bird gave her a haughty glance and remarked:

'Dinner is served in the small ballroom, your grace.'

'Ain't he a stunner?' Nate said. 'He goes on like that all the time. We reckoned as how he musta belonged to some lord or duke once.'

'Order the perch phaeton,' croaked Mr Jenkins. 'A young person has called, your lordship. Tea is served in her grace's boudoir. Ho, there, a chair for Lady Fothergill!'

'You silly old sausage,' said Nate, giving his pet a loving hug. 'There aren't any lords or dukes here.'

Affronted and on his dignity, Mr Jenkins clambered out of Nate's arms and ascended to the top of his head, where he suddenly shouted in a stentorian voice, 'God save the King! Hooray for Jamie Three! God save our sovereign lord King James and DOWN WITH THE GEORGIANS!'

Mr Slighcarp happened to be passing at that moment. He gave a violent start and dropped the telescope he was carrying. It fell with a crash.

'Who said that?' he cried.

'It was the bird, Mr Slighcarp, old Jenkins.'

'Well don't let him do it again or I'll wring his neck!' the mate said with an oath. 'Plague take the creature, you'd best keep him under hatches if he's liable to go on like that. I won't have it, see?'

Much abashed, Nate hurried his pet below. Dido, who was still feeling wakeful, retreated to a patch of shadow against the bulwarks and curled up there, listening longingly to cheerful sounds of music and singing from the *Martha*.

Presently Captain Casket approached her. He was a changed man; his eyes glittered feverishly and he walked with a rapid, excited step.

'Ah, my child,' he said cordially. 'Is not this stirring news?'

Dido thought he was referring to the mail he had received.

'You fixed up what you're going to do about young Pen, then, when you gets back to Nantucket?' she said hopefully. 'Someone offered to look arter her?'

'Oh, that. No, no. Captain Bilger tells me that the pink whale has been sighted off the Peruvian coast. We shall see her! I feel certain that we shall see her soon!'

'Oh, bother the pink whale,' Dido said testily. 'What about Pen?'

'Ah yes. Dear Tribulation writes with true sisterly feeling, having just heard of my poor wife's death. She will move to Nantucket and look after Dutiful Penitence and the house for me.'

'But, blame it!' Dido said in exasperation. 'Pen don't *want* to live with her Auntie Tribulation! On account of summat her ma said she's scared to death of the notion; it won't answer at *all*! Can't you get that into your seaweedy noddle?'

'She suggests further,' Captain Casket went on, dreamily looking out over the water and ignoring Dido, 'that a companion, some other girl of her age, would be an advantage for Penitence, since my farm, Soul's Hill, is situated in a somewhat lonely location. So if thee will accept the charge, my child, not for very long, of course, that will solve all our problems, will it not? Thy quick wit will soon smooth over any little difficulties between my daughter and her good aunt. And when Penitence is settled and happy, my sister Tribulation will no doubt see that thee is found a passage to England. Remember, too, that we rescued thee from the sea, my child, and that thee owes us a debt of gratitude.'

Silenced for the moment, Dido scowled after him as he walked away. An hour or so went by and she was about to retire when she noticed the figure of Mr Slighcarp standing not far away. Something furtive and cautious about his manner attracted her interest and she watched him sharply as he made his way to the rail. Unaware of Dido, squatting motionless in the shadows, Mr Slighcarp looked quickly all round him and then proceeded to tear in tiny pieces some sheets of paper which he had carried hidden in the breast of his jacket and drop them over the side.

'What's he doing that for?' wondered Dido. 'What's so tarnation private about a letter?'

Then she recalled that Mr Slighcarp had been asked to collect a letter for the captain, and that he had not done so. He had said Captain Bilger had made a mistake, the letter was for somebody else. Was it possible that he had lied?

Could the letter really have been for Captain Casket after all? Suppose this was it? But why should he be destroying it?

There seemed no answer to this puzzle, or none that Dido could supply. She continued to watch Mr Slighcarp attentively, however, and was somewhat astonished by what he did next. Making sure, as he thought, that he was unobserved, he produced a pair of boots from under his jacket, and brushed them long and carefully.

Dido's heart beat fast and she nodded to herself grimly.

A brilliant tropical moon swam overhead and by its light, and that of a pewter lantern not far away, every detail of the scene was clearly visible. The boots that Mr Slighcarp brushed were no sailors' brogans, but a pair of English ladies' buttoned travelling-boots in dull bottle-green.

At last, satisfied, apparently, with the appearance of the boots, Mr Slighcarp retired once more, in the same prudent and furtive manner.

Dido remained on deck for a considerable time longer. At first she had half a mind to tell Captain Casket about the incident. But then she decided not to. After all, what had she to go on but suspicion; who could say that the letter was not Mr Slighcarp's own? He had every right to tear up his own letter. Furthermore, if Mr Slighcarp realized that Dido had seen him tear it up, he would know that she had also seen him brushing the boots. He would be revealed as the accomplice of the stowaway lady in the blubber-room. Dido had not forgotten this lady's fiercely whispered threat, 'Keep a still tongue in your head. Otherwise your chances of ever seeing London River again are very, very small!'

'I'll keep mum,' she finally decided. 'After all, if I did tell Captain Casket, like as not he'd only gaze at me in that moon-faced way o' his and start to talk about his everlasting pink whale. I dessay it wasn't his letter. And I don't

want an up-and-a-downer with old man Slighcarp. I'll keep a still tongue. But I'll watch.'

Nate, whose turn it was on the middle watch, came on deck at this moment, and passed the time of night with Dido. Mr Jenkins, sitting on his shoulder, gave a polite croak, and remarked:

'Your lordship's bath is ready in the tapestry room. I have warmed the morning paper, Sir Henry. Pray bring his grace's bath-chair this way. Down with the scurvy Hanoverians!'

'Best watch out for Mr Slighcarp,' Dido said grinning.

'No danger, it's his watch below,' Nate said. 'That's why I brought old Jenkins up for a breath of air.'

'I wonder why he riles Mr Slighcarp so,' Dido said yawning.

'Don't you know? Because Mr Slighcarp's English too, but he was a Hanoverian, on the other side. He wanted to get rid of that king you got. So he don't like it when the old bird says "Down with the Hanoverians". He had to run aboard in a hurry or he'd a been clapped in prison, the militia was after him. Leastways, that's what Uncle 'Lije said. Mr Slighcarp hasn't shipped with Cap'n Casket very long, but he stayed in Nantucket a piece before that.'

'He's English? Mr Slighcarp?'

'Sure. You'd think he'd a taken a bit more of a shine to you,' Nate said, 'seeing you both come from the same part.'

It was a long time, almost dawn, before Dido fell asleep, and when she did so her slumbers were soon broken short by a sudden shout and violent disturbance.

The whole ship seemed to give a tremendous bound, like a startled horse; there were loud and prolonged cries overhead; feet thudded on the deck and Dido heard the crash and rattle as sails were shaken out and the anchor was dragged bodily from the bottom.

'What's the matter, what's happened?' Pen cried fearfully – she had been jerked out of bed by the ship's un-expected movement and was whimpering on the floor. 'Is it a hurricane?'

Dido held up a hand for silence. She was listening atten-tively to the shouts overhead.

'No,' she said dryly after a minute. 'It ain't a hurricane; a little thing like that wouldn't get your pa so stirred-up. Oh, well, one thing, it'll help us on our way home at a rattling good pace. That is, allus supposing the old gal plays her part and don't go skedaddling off to Timbuctoo or Tobago.'

'How do you mean? What old gal?'

'Why,' Dido said, 'the pink 'un. Rosie Lee. Hear what they shouted? We're a-chasin' after that there sweet-pea-coloured whale of his'n.'

The days and weeks that followed were fierce and rug-ged. Careering after her quarry through the South Pacific Trades, the *Sarah Casket* flew along under every sail that she would take. Main-tops, top-gallants, and stunsails were set, the rigging thrummed like a banjo, and often, as they drove through the southern seas, their mainmast was bent over so far that Nate declared they might as well use it for a bow, if they ever got close enough to the pink whale, and fire off a harpoon from the mainstay.

Nothing would persuade Penitence on deck now, and even Dido, when they reached the wild easterlies and heavy squalls in the straits of Magellan, was glad enough to stay in the cabin playing pachisi.

At first Dido was inclined, like the others, to believe that Captain Casket had merely imagined his glimpse of the pink whale at Galapagos, until one evening, south of Cape Horn, she saw something between two wildly blowing williwaws that she at first took to be a momentary view of the setting sun – except that it lay to the east. It was like a rosy, iridescent bubble balanced amid the black, leaping seas. Then the storm came down again and they saw it no more. But Captain Casket, with a frantic, exultant light in his eye, kept the ship under a full press of canvas, heedless of danger, clapping on new sails as the old ones ripped away. Without regard to tempest, tidal wave, or terremoto, he fought his way round the Horn, making a record passage of it, while his men served four hours on and four off, becoming haggard and thin from wear and tear and lack of sleep. The captain himself never seemed to sleep at all and his eyes were red from scanning the horizon.

There were few chances for Nate to come down to the cabin now; he was kept busy all the time as a lookout, or taking soundings, or mending the tattered sails. Sometimes he could be heard singing as he sewed, with Mr Jenkins (who had acquired a wholesome respect for Mr Slighcarp) supplying the chorus in a subdued croak:

> 'Stow your line-tubs, belay tail-feathers,
> It's rough, it's rugged, it's blowy weather.
> Make your passage and follow the moon –
> *Dinner is served in the blue saloon.*
>
> 'Slush the spars and splice the rigging
> Leave your scrimshaw and grab your piggin
> Bail, boys, bail! for your wage and lay –
> *Her ladyship's carriage blocks the way.*'

Mr Jenkins spent a good deal of this time with the girls in the cabin; Nate was glad to know that his pet was in a safe spot, and the girls were glad of the company, particularly as Mr Jenkins made an extremely civil guest. He would play tiddlywinks (if ever they struck a long enough patch of calm weather), flipping scrimshaw counters into a cup with great dexterity and enjoyment; while his grave observations about life in high society kept Pen and Dido amused for hours.

Past Trinidad they chased, past the Brazilian coast,

through the Sargasso Sea (which slowed down the pink whale a little, for she got weeds caught in her flukes), past Bermuda, past Cape Hatteras, and so home. But the pink whale, unfortunately, seemed disinclined to stop, and mutterings were to be heard among the men that at this rate they'd likely be skating past Newfoundland before they discharged cargo and had their pay.

A deputation waited on Captain Casket and pointed out to him that they were low on stores and water, that there wasn't a single unmended sail on board and that what hardtack was left would walk away from you along the deck if you let go of your ration for a moment. With great difficulty he was persuaded to put in to New Bedford.

And so it was that, almost seven months to the day after she had first opened her eyes on board the *Sarah Casket*, Dido had a chance to set foot on solid ground.

'New Bedford!' she said ungratefully. 'Where's that, I ask you? Land sakes, Cap'n Casket mighta just as well nipped across to Dover, it wouldn't a taken him but a few more weeks.'

She glared with disfavour at the trim roofs of the town climbing its hill above the harbour. 'Still,' she admitted in acknowledgement of the forest of masts, 'I will say there's a-plenty o' shipping here; maybe I'll find some bark as'll take me on to England.'

'You promised you'd come home with me first, you *promised*,' Pen reminded her anxiously.

'All right, all right, I ain't forgotten,' Dido growled. 'I've said I'll see you right and I will – if we can only get your pa to tend to your affairs for two minutes together. You know you had a notion your cousin Ann Allerton might put you up.'

Captain Casket hardly even attended to the business of getting his ship safely docked. His eyes were constantly turned back towards the open sea, and his thoughts were all with the pink whale, who had unfairly taken the chance to

63

nip off round Cape Cod and into the Gulf of Maine. Would he ever catch up with her again?

It was dark before the *Sarah Casket* was alongside the wharf and made fast. Penitence begged to go ashore then and there, but Captain Casket wouldn't hear of disturbing Cousin Ann Allerton so late in the evening, and left them to spend one more night on board. Dido stayed awake for hours, sniffing the land-smells, listening to the shouts and the splash of oars in the harbour and the cry of gulls, and the music coming from the sailors' taverns. She dragged a chair to the port and squatted there looking out at the lights as they gradually dimmed and died along the wharfside and in the streets above the warehouses.

Strangely enough, although she was now nearer home than she had been for the last year, she felt more lonely and homesick than ever before.

'Pen!' she whispered after a while. 'Hey, Dutiful! Are you awake?'

The only answer was soft, even breathing. Dido sighed, and was about to climb down from her perch and go to bed, when she heard a faint splash, close to, and the creak of oars. Turning back, she was just in time to see Mr Slighcarp, his foxy features visible in the light of a lantern, help a tall, veiled woman over the *Sarah Casket*'s side into a dory, and row quietly away across the harbour.

PART TWO

5

*Trouble with Cousin Ann – Captain Casket slips his cable –
arrival in Nantucket – the Casket farm*

'WE can't stay with your cousin Allerton,' Dido said
glumly, 'and *that's* for sure.'

It had taken her less than ten minutes to reach this
conclusion. After ten days she was of the same mind.

Cousin Ann Allerton was a frail, erect old lady dressed in
black silk with a white bib and cap. She almost fainted
when her snapping black eyes first took in the untidy
appearance of the two girls – even Pen's dress was fairly
bedraggled by this time with oil and tar on its frills. And as
for Dido – !

'Don't stand on the clean doormat!' Cousin Ann said
frantically. 'Keziah! Keziah! Fetch an old sheet directly
and put on a pail of water to heat. Mercy! Just look at that
child's feet! And her *hair*! Bring some towels, every stitch
they have on will have to be burned. Get out the tallow and
kerosene, gracious knows how we are going to get that
grease off. Fetch the sulphur and calomel, I don't doubt
they need a good dose after eating dear knows what
foreign truck on board ship. And when you've done that,
run down the road and ask Miss Alsop to step up, they'll
have to have everything new, I can see that – furs, flannels,
merinos, poplins, and tarlatans. Bonnets, of course, and
boots; mercy on us what a pair of little savages.'

'I'd ruther keep my britches,' Dido said scowling.

'Quiet, child! The idea! Pass me the bath-brick,
Keziah, till I give them a good scrubbing.'

Dido had never been so treated in her life before and was
almost too thunderstruck to protest; in no time they were

put to bed in a spotlessly neat bedroom with white chintz curtains and fringed white dimity bedcovers, a braided rug exactly in the middle of the floor and a square of oilcloth in front of the wash-stand.

'Why've we got to go to bed in daytime?' grumbled Dido. 'We ain't done nothing wrong!'

'Oh, for the land's sake, will you hold your hush. You must stay out of sight of the neighbours till you've something fit to wear.'

Miss Alsop the dressmaker soon arrived, and with Cousin Ann's help two brown calico dresses trimmed with white tape were hastily run up so that the children might put them on, get out of bed, and help to hem some more garments.

'I won't stand for it,' Dido muttered again and again, wriggling her neck furiously in her starched collar as she sewed under Cousin Ann's gimlet-eyed supervision. The only respite they had from sewing was when the gaunt and gloomy maid Keziah compelled them to swallow another dose of rhubarb or senna or sassefras tea; Cousin Ann seemed quite certain that they had brought the plague with them from abroad and must be physicked at frequent intervals to prevent it from spreading through the town.

Even Captain Casket was mildly surprised at the transformation in the two children when he came to call. Dido badly wanted to tackle hin about the possibility of finding a home for Pen other than with Aunt Tribulation, and about her own passage to England, but he paid only a brief visit and never came near Cousin Ann's house again, so busy was he with refitting and reprovisioning the ship, and asking all newcomers for news of the pink whale. Meanwhile the children were kept under strict supervision; only allowed out for a short walk once a day, to the end of the road and back.

However, on the ninth day while Keziah was at a missionary meeting, Cousin Ann found herself obliged to lie down with a headache brought on, she said, by the trampling of children's feet upstairs in the bedroom. No sooner had she retired than Dido was out of the house like a bullet.

'*You* can stay, Pen, if you're scared to come,' she said, 'but I wants to see your pa and get things fixed up shipshape.'

Pen said she would remain at home in case Cousin Ann needed anything, so Dido flew down the hill to the wharfside. What was her horror, when she reached the berth that had been the *Sarah Casket*'s, to find it empty!

'Hey,' she said to a boy who was fishing near by, 'where's the ship that was here?'

'Sailed this morning on the early tide.'

'She didn't! You're bamming!'

He shrugged. 'What d'you think she did, then? Walked away up the hill? The old skipper was raring to go – someone told him they'd seen a pink whale off Gay Head. He was missing his first mate when he sailed but he said he couldn't wait, so he up anchor and off; guess he's halfway to the Grand Banks b'now.'

'Oh, croopus,' groaned Dido. She turned and walked wearily back up the steep hill; her legs felt as heavy as lead. 'Now we are in the basket! What an old chiseller Cap'n Casket is; I mighta knowed he'd play us a trick like that – sneaking off on the quiet so's Pen couldn't make a fuss, I'll lay! One thing's certain, though – I ain't a-goin to stop any longer with Cousin Ann.'

Luckily Cousin Ann was of the same mind. She had had the forethought to collect money for their fares to Nantucket from Captain Casket when he called, and the very next day they were dispatched, with their new clothes, on the packet *Adelaide*, a small schooner loaded up to her eyebrows with coal, cordwood, and water-melons.

A rising gale delayed the crossing considerably, and dusk had fallen by the time the ship rounded Brant Point and came safe into Nantucket harbour. Salty, soaked, and shivering, the girls clambered on to the wharf with their bundles. 'Hey!' the captain called into the gloom. 'Anyone here from the Casket place?'

Nobody answered. The two children waited for some time, until most of the other passengers, or people unloading goods from the packet, had left.

'Well, it ain't no manner of use standing here all night,' Dido said, clenching her teeth to prevent their chattering. 'And it ain't half a-going to rain in a minute. What'll us do, Pen? Can we walk to your pa's farm? Is it far?'

'N-nine miles,' shivered Pen. 'It's much too far to walk with our bundles.'

'Had us better put up at an inn?'

'Oh, no! They're sure to be full of horrid rough sailors.'

'Well I ain't stopping here,' Dido said, and led the way into Nantucket town with Pen following irresolutely. 'Maybe we'll see somebody you know if we wander a bit; maybe your Auntie Trib reckoned the packet warn't coming and went shopping or started home again. I can tell you one thing, I'm crabbish hungry,' she added, as they passed a chowder parlour and a heart-breaking smell of food drifted out to them.

'Oh, so am I!'

'Got any money?'

'Why, no,' faltered Penitence. 'Cousin Ann only gave me the boat tickets.'

'Hum,' Dido said. She hefted her bundle thoughtfully. Just ahead of them, on the corner of Main and Union streets, was a store with windows still brightly lit up and a sign that said: 'Bracy and Starbuck, Ships' Outfitters and General Soft Goods'.

'I'm a-going in here,' Dido said, and did so, ignoring Pen's apprehensive squeak. She addressed herself to a man behind the counter.

'Hey, mister, I've got a load of clobber here that I don't want, will you buy it off me?'

To Pen's horror the man was quite prepared to buy the carefully-made dresses and frilly underwear considered suitable by Cousin Ann. 'What do I want with 'em?' Dido said. 'I'd sooner have a pair of britches any day.' She bought herself a red flannel shirt and a pair of denim trousers for one dollar sixty-two cents, and still had two dollars left. 'Come on, Pen,' she said, 'we'll go get us some prog. By the way,' she asked the outfitter, 'you don't know if there's anybody in town a-waiting for Miss Pen Casket, does you?'

'Little Miss Casket for the Casket farm?' he said. 'Why yes, the old mule's been in every day this week. Guess he's still around; Mr Hussey at the Grampus Inn knows not to loose him till the packet's been in an hour. Are you little Miss Casket then? My, how you have growed!'

Dido didn't wait to chat. 'Which way's the Grampus Inn?' she asked. 'Come on, Pen, hurry!' Slipping and stumbling, they ran along the cobbled streets, scaring a number of sheep who appeared to have come into the town to take shelter, and reached a building with a wildly swinging sign that showed a grampus in full spout. Below the sign was tethered a mule-cart; the dejected mule, his coat sleek with rain, seemed to be trying to keep his head dry by hiding it between his forelegs.

'Is that your pa's cart?' asked Dido.

'I – I'm not sure,' Penitence confessed. 'It's such a long time since I was at home. There *was* a mule – I think he was called Mungo – but I used to be scared of him, I never noticed what he was like.'

'Oy,' said Dido, going round to the mule's front end. 'Psst, you! Hey! Is your name Mungo?'

The mule made no response, except to give her a despising glance from one white-rimmed eye, backwards, between his legs.

'I'm going in to ask,' Dido said.

'Oh dear, I'm sure you shouldn't go into an inn!' Pen

lamented. 'There will be dreadful people. It isn't ladylike behaviour!'

'Oh, *scrape* ladylike behaviour!' Dido snapped impatiently. 'If you want to get soaked and starved, *I* don't!'

She marched into the inn. Having ascertained that it was indeed Captain Casket's mule and cart standing outside, she said: 'Well, if he's waited for us every day this week it won't kill him to wait another twenty minutes,' and to Pen's fright she ordered three bowls of clam chowder. However, the chowder was so welcome when it came, savoury and hot, full of tender little clams, that Pen at length overcame her qualms and consented to eat it.

'Who's the third bowl for?' she asked.

'Why, poor old Mungo, o' course,' Dido said reprovingly. 'If he's got nine miles to go through the wet he ought to have summat to stay his stomach.'

'Will he like it?' Pen quavered.

'We'll soon see, won't us? If he don't, I dessay you can do with a second help.'

However, the mule seemed quite willing to accept a helping of chowder and appeared to improve greatly in his spirits once he had snuffled it down. The dish was returned to the inn. Dido helped Pen into the cart and wrapped her in a quantity of sheepskins which were found under the seat. Then she untied Mungo's head, slapped him with the reins, and they were off.

'Whizzo!' she said, as they rattled through the dimly lit streets. 'This is something like, ain't it? I loves drivin' – if only it didn't rain and blow *quite* so hard. I say, Pen, does you know the way?'

'Mungo knows it, I dare say,' said Pen faintly – she had soon left the box and was huddled down in the bottom of the cart trying to keep herself from slipping about. 'Mamma used to send him in to market on his own with the eggs and stuff. Just give him his head, he'll find his way home.'

In no time they were out of the little town and making their way along a high and exposed sandy track in open country. The wind and rain buffeted them and it was too dark to see anything except some low-growing shrubs by the roadside. A distant, continuous roar could be heard to their right, and from ahead of them came louder, but inter-mittent booming.

'What's all that row?' Dido said.

'It's the waves.'

'But we've just come from the sea.'

'Nantucket's an island, don't forget,' Pen sighed drearily. 'What you can hear is the breakers on the south and east shores. Oh, how I hate it!'

'Now, *Pen*, cheer up, do!' Dido said. 'How about a song to keep ourselves cheerful, one o' Nate's?' And she began to sing in a hoarse but tuneful voice:

> 'Oh, fierce is the Ocean and wild is the Sound,
> But the isle of Nantucket is where I am bound,
> Sweet isle of Nantucket! where the grapes are so red,
> And the light flashes nightly on Sankaty Head!'

Inspired by this, Mungo the mule actually broke into a canter and so they went briskly on their way through the storm.

'Hey,' said Dido, at last, 'Pen, here's a gate. Croopus, did you ever see sich a peculiar one? Is this your pa's place?'

'I think so,' Pen sighed faintly, peering forward in the gloom. 'Yes, he put up the gate; it is made of a sperm-whale's jawbone. Oh, I am so cold and wet and miserable.'

'Ne'mind, in ten minutes you'll be tucked in bed with a warming-pan. There's a barn, anyhows; Mungo seems to think he lives here.'

In fact, after they had passed the gate, which was like an enormous wish-bone, Mungo trotted into the big barn without worrying any further about his human passengers;

Penitence was rather impatient when Dido insisted on un-
harnessing him and giving him a rub with a wisp of hay,
'Just in case,' she said, 'your Auntie Trib don't fancy
stepping out into the wet. All right, come on now, bring
your traps.'

There appeared to be quite a group of farm buildings set
in a hollow of the hillside with a few trees round about. Not
a light showed anywhere and it was hard to be sure which
was the dwelling-house.

At last they found what seemed to be a house door and
Pen, a sudden memory returning from earlier childhood,
stood on tiptoe and discovered a key hanging on a nail.

'Hooroar,' Dido said as they stepped inside. 'Ain't I glad
to get in out o' the wet. Know where the candles is kept,
Pen?'

'N-no, I forget,' Pen said dolefully. 'Oh, isn't it dark and cold!'

Luckily, feeling about, Dido chanced to knock over a candle; when it was restored and lit they saw that they were in a large, old-fashioned kitchen which, given warmth and light, would have been a cheerful place enough. There was a big potbellied stove, black, unlit, and unwelcoming; a brightly-coloured braided rug, and a dresser covered with dishes. An enormous grandfather clock ticked solemnly against the wall. The place was clean and tidy but silent, empty, and deathly cold.

'Oh,' whispered Pen. 'What shall we do now?'

'Do? Why, go to bed. Things'll be better in the morning,' Dido said stoutly. 'Where's the stairs?'

Pen opened a door disclosing a steep narrow flight, and Dido went ahead with the candle.

'Hey,' she said, checking to let Pen catch up, 'look, there's a light under that door at the end o' the passage. Must be your Auntie Trib's room. We'd better go and tell her we've come.'

'B-b-but,' whispered Pen tremulously, 'supposing it *isn't* her?'

She clutched Dido's arm.

'Why, you sapskull! Who else could it be? Come on!'

Dido marched boldly along the passage and rapped on the door.

'Miss Casket?' she called. 'It's us – Penitence and Dido, just arrived.'

From the room beyond a voice replied, 'And about time, too! Wipe your feet on the mat before you come in.'

Even Dido quailed momentarily at the sound of this voice. It was low, harsh, and grating; there was something very forbidding, and something strangely familiar about it. Her hand trembled slightly and she spilled a drop of hot wax from the candle which went out; then, summoning resolution, she pushed open the door and went in.

By the light of one dim candle on the bedside table they could see a woman in the bed, propped against many pillows, regarding them fixedly.

6

Aunt Tribulation – pigs and sheep –
green boots in the attic – Aunt Tribulation is hungry –
Pen meets a stranger

'LIGHT another candle,' ordered the woman in the bed, 'and let's have a look at you. Hum,' she said to Dido, 'you don't favour my side of the family. Must take after that poor sickly Sarah.'

'You got it wrong, ma'am,' Dido said hastily. 'That's Pen there. I'm Dido Twite.'

Although she stared at the girls pretty sharply, it was hard for them to see much of Pen's aunt, for she held the bedclothes up to her chin, and had on a nightcap with a wide frill that left most of her face in shadow. They could just make out a gaunt, nutcracker chin, and a thin nose, so like a ship's rudder that Dido half expected it to move from side to side. A pair of tinted glasses hid Aunt Tribulation's eyes from view. Dido grinned, thinking of the wolf, and subdued an urge to exclaim: 'Why, Auntie Trib, what big eyes you have!'

'*You're* a pasty-faced little bag of bones,' Aunt Tribulation commented, looking at Pen. 'Haven't filled out as you grew, have you? Well, I hope you're both used to hard work, that's all. You'll get no lounging and pampering here.' She thumped on the floor with a rubber-shod stick to emphasize her words. 'There's all the house chores and the farm work; *I* can't help you, as I've been sick abed ever since I got here; this damp island air turns a body's bones to corkscrews. So you'd best get to bed now.'

'Where shall we sleep, Aunt Trib?' Dido asked.

'In the chamber at the other end of the passage. Sheets

and blankets are in the cedarwood box. Mrs Pardon's been coming over to tend the animals, but you'll have to do them now. Feed the hens and pigs at four, groom the mule. Light the stove – you'll need to chop some kindling if there's none in the cellar; and the peat's in the peat-house – and you càn bring me a pot of coffee and a bowl of gruel at seven. Look sharp now.'

Too dazed by the length of this list of tasks to make any protest, the girls retreated, and found their room which was as bleak and clean as at Cousin Ann's, but lacking the wash-stand, square of oilcloth, and braid rug. Shivering and yawning they dragged comforters and sheets from the cedar box, made up the bed, and tumbled into it, huddling against one another for warmth.

'I'm that tired I could sleep for a week o' Thursdays,' Dido murmured drowsily. 'Dear knows how we'll ever wake at four.'

Pen was asleep already, but Dido lay for a moment trying to think why Aunt Tribulation's voice had sounded so familiar. Then she too fell deep asleep.

She need not have worried about how they were to wake; there were three roosters on the farm whose lusty crowing had the girls roused long before any touch of dawn had crossed the sky. Dressing themselves hastily in warm things – Dido put on the denims and red shirt she had bought – they groped their way downstairs.

They lit the potbellied stove, staggered in from the pump with a bucket of water between them, fed the animals, and were just making the gruel when a loud thumping on the floor overhead proclaimed that Aunt Tribulation was awake. Pen went up to see what she wanted and was greeted with the words:

'Where's my breakfast? You're ten minutes late.'

'I – I'm very sorry, Aunt Tribulation.'

'Sorry! Sorry's not good enough. Don't forget to scald the coffee pot. And clear the coffee with eggshells. And when you've brought me my breakfast and washed the dishes and towels, you can scrub the kitchen floor and dust the parlour. Then you'll have to make some bread. And that other girl can hoe the potato field.'

'Huh,' Dido said when this programme was unfolded to her. 'Don't she want us to cut down no trees? Or slap a few bricks together and put up a new barn? Anyhows I'm a-going to have some breakfast before I start on that lot. Here, I'll take up the old girl's prog, Pen; I've fried you some eggs; sit down and get 'em inside you, you look like a bit o' cheesecloth.'

Aunt Tribulation received her breakfast tray without enthusiasm. 'Wash your face before you come up another time, girl,' she said harshly. 'And where's my napkin? You should have used the pink china, this is kitchen stuff.'

'Lookahere, you ungrateful old cuss,' burst out Dido, her patience at an end, 'you oughta be thankful I didn't bring it up in a baking-pan! Lord bless us, am I glad you ain't *my* Aunt Trib.'

She ran out of the room, slamming the door behind her.

To Dido's great surprise and relief, Pen proved a handy little creature with the indoor tasks; she had been taught by her mother to wash and bake and cook and polish; 'which it's as well,' Dido admitted, 'for I never could abide housework and I don't know a waffle-iron from a skillet; if I'd a had to make the bread it'd turn out tougher'n old boots. It beats all how you get it to rise so, Pen. You'll have to teach me; one thing, housework ain't so bad when it's just us on our own. In fact it's quite a lark. Pity the old gal couldn't go back to wherever she came from.'

'Oh Dido,' confessed Pen – they were out of earshot of Aunt Tribulation now, sociably hoeing the enormous potato field together, 'she frightens me *dreadfully*! Her eyes glare so – at least I'm sure they do behind her glasses! And her voice is so angry and scolding. I'm sure I shall never get used to her.'

'Now, now, Pen,' Dido admonished. 'Remember as how you're learning to be brave? Every morning when you get up you must say twenty times, "I am not scared of Auntie Trib." You'd best start now.'

'I am not scared of Auntie Trib,' Pen said obediently. But then she broke out, 'It's no use, Dido, I *am* scared of her!'

'Well, we'll have to get you out o' the habit,' Dido said stoutly. 'You watch me, see how I stand up to the old sulphur-bottom.'

Pen gulped, nodding, but she looked apprehensive.

'Do you remember her now you see her again, Penny?' Dido asked. 'Is she like she was when you was small?'

'Just as frightening,' Pen said. 'But I don't really remember her much. It was Mamma saying she was a dragon that I remembered. She looks older than I expected. And even crosser!'

Dido pondered over Pen's words. Really, she thought, there's nothing to prove that this lady is Aunt Tribulation at all. This is a mouldy lookout for me getting back to England; I don't see leaving Pen with old Gruff-and-Grumble.

She thought this again when the noon hour came and they entered the house to the accompaniment of a regular hurricane of thumps from upstairs. Pen ran up to inquire her aunt's wishes and returned trembling and in tears, so fierce had been the request for 'gingerbread and apple sauce and look sharp about it, miss! What have you been doing all morning, I'd like to know? Idling and playing and picking flowers, I suppose!'

'Oh, pray don't scold, Aunt Tribulation, pray don't. Indeed, indeed, we haven't been idling; we have hoed more than half the potato field.'

'Old harridan. I wonder how she knew you'd made some gingerbread?' Dido said. 'She must have a nose on her like a bloodhound. There's some apples down cellar, Penny, I saw them when I was getting the kindling for the stove. And there's hams and onions and molasses and bushels of beans, so we shan't starve and nor will old Mortification upstairs.'

As Pen hurried to get the apples Dido, stoking the stove, muttered, 'Ill, my eye! If she's so ill, what's her nightcap ribbon doing on the kitchen floor? You've been poking and snooping and spying, you old madam, you, to see whether we did the housework, you horrid old hypocrite!'

When the apple sauce was made she took a saucerful up to Aunt Tribulation with the cap ribbon ostentatiously stuck like an ornament at the side of the dish. 'I guess this is yours, Auntie Trib,' she remarked innocently. 'I can't *think* how it come to be lying on the floor downstairs. Acos you haven't been down, have you?'

Aunt Tribulation took this very much amiss. 'Impertinent girl! Don't speak to me in that way. Apologize immediately!'

'Why should I?' Dido said reasonably. 'You ain't been extra polite to us.'

'You shall be shut up in the attic till you learn better manners.'

'Tally-ho! I'm agreeable,' said Dido. 'I can jistabout do with a nap arter all that hoeing.'

'Not now,' said Aunt Tribulation, who appeared suddenly to recollect that she had other plans for the girls. 'I want you and Penitence to shift the sheep up to the high pasture. And mind you count them! Do that as soon as you've washed the dishes. And don't forget to make up the stove. And feed the hens and pigs.'

'Sure that's all?' inquired Dido. 'Nothing else as how you can lay your mind to? Sartin? Tooralooral, then.'

'Now, how the mischief are we to count these here blame sheep?' Dido said, as the girls walked down the sandy lane to the pasture where the sheep were grazing.

'There's a gate in those railings over there,' Pen said. 'If you could get behind them and drive them, I could count them as they came through.'

'Clever girl, Pen. You've got a right smart head on your shoulders when you doesn't get all of a-pucker and a-fluster.'

Dido ran off across the rough pasture which was not grass but low-growing scraggy shrubs and bushes. Pen waited by the gate, and, conquering a slight tendency to shrink in alarm as the sheep streamed towards her, manfully counted them.

'Two hundred and twenty-three,' she said when they were all through and being driven up towards the high pasture. 'I wonder if that is the right number?'

'Well if it ain't you may lay Auntie Trib will tell us fast enough. Croopus, don't the wind blow up here, and can't we see a long way!'

'All over the island,' Pen said wanly, looking across the rolling, shrubby moorlands to the line of the ocean. On the south shore white, mushrooming clouds of spray from breakers could be seen dimly through a belt of haze.

'What's that white tower to the east?'

'Sankaty Head lighthouse. There's a forest between us and it,' Pen said with a faint glimmer of pride, 'but you can't see it. It's called the Hidden Forest. That's uncommon, isn't it?'

'Rummy,' agreed Dido. 'So's your pa's house. Why's it got a balcony on the roof? And why's it standing on legs?'

'I don't know about the legs. The balcony was for Mamma so she could look out to sea and see if Papa's ship was in sight. Look, isn't that a man coming to call at the house? We'd better go home.'

'Race you down the hill,' Dido said, and was astonished when Pen nodded, picked up her skirts, and darted away down the sandy track.

But when they reached the house, panting and laughing, nobody seemed to be about. The man had vanished. They ran into the kitchen, and Dido went up to Aunt Tribulation's room.

'Is somebody called here?' she asked, knocking and entering. There was a sort of flurry from the bed, as Aunt Tribulation huddled down in her pillows. Two spots of crimson showed on her thin cheeks.

'Do not come in until I give you leave, miss!' she croaked.

'Sorry, I'm sure! We was feared you mighta had to get up and answer the door.'

'I have done no such thing! Be off to your work!'

'Good land, don't be in such a pelter. I'm just a-going,' Dido said, injured. But in the passage outside she paused, remembering that the door next to Aunt Tribulation's opened on an upward flight of stairs. Must lead to that fancy balcony, she thought. I've a good mind to step up, won't take but a moment. She tried the door. Strangely enough it was locked now, though she was sure it had been open before.

'Why are you loitering out there, girl?' Aunt Tribulation called angrily from her room.

Dido shrugged and ran downstairs.

'Does that door by Aunt Trib's room lead up to the roof, Penny?' she asked.

'Yes, and to the attic.'

'Where's the key kept?'

'In the door, mostly,' Pen said in surprise. 'But there's a spare, because once when I was little I locked myself in there. Oh, I was scared, and so was Mamma!'

'Where's the spare live, then?'

'On a hook at the back of the china closet. Why?'

'Just I've a fancy to go up there sometime,' Dido replied calmly. She did not add that she was also curious to know what Aunt Tribulation was up to: it seemed clear that while the girls were out she had locked the attic door and taken the key. Why had she done so?

'What'll us do now, Penny?' she inquired.

'I suppose we're free,' Pen said doubtfully. 'I'd like to do some lessons. And write my journal and sew my sampler.'

'Not on your Oliphant. There's the old gal a-thumping again.'

Aunt Tribulation called imperiously for Pen to bring her more gingerbread and apple sauce.

'How many sheep did you count?' she demanded.

'Two hundred and twenty-three, Aunt Tribulation,' Pen quavered.

'One missing! That one must be found, miss.'

'Y-y-yes, Aunt!'

'Make haste and set about it, then.'

Pen bore up till she was downstairs, but then she burst into tears.

'Oh, I'm so tired! And look, it's nearly dark outside. Do you think we really need go tonight, Dido? I'm sure we'd never find it. And I don't believe I can walk another step.'

'Nor you shall,' said Dido sturdily. 'Be blowed to the old faggot. How does she expect us to find one sheep in the dark in umpty miles o' wild country? That's a crazy notion. It'll look after itself till morning, I reckon; we'll find it then. Run along to bed, Pen, while I stoke the stove and lock the back door.'

Pen was already half asleep by the time Dido tiptoed up and snuggled in beside her under the quilted comforters.

'I brought the back and front door keys,' she whispered, tucking them under the pillow. 'Just so's to be on the safe side. 'Night, Dutiful. You'll have to write a letter to your pa about all this.'

'Good night, Dido. Yes, I will write a letter.'

Halfway through the night Dido woke up and lay listening sharply. This ain't half a creaky old house, she thought. Every pine board seemed to have its own separate voice, and when the wind blew it was almost like being on the ship. But no wind was blowing now, and yet a board had creaked. Burglars? Dido slid a hand under the pillow and satisfied herself that both keys were still there. Pen slept peacefully. The creak was not repeated and, after a while, Dido too drifted back into sleep and dreamed that she was asking Aunt Tribulation to lend her the fare to England, while Pen weepingly begged her not to go, and Aunt Tribulation made no reply except to shake her red wattles, wink a black, beady eye, and croak, 'Certainly not! Certainly not! Get up, you lazy girl! Cock-a-doodle-doo!'

'Wake up, Pen, it's morning.'

'Oh, no, it can't be!' moaned Pen. 'I could sleep for hours longer.'

'Never mind. At least we shan't have to light the stove this morning. I can jistabout do with some bacon and coffee.'

They dressed in the warm kitchen. While Dido was brushing Pen's long hair, Pen said, 'That's odd. I thought we left the window fastened. Look, it's only pushed to.'

Dido considered the window in frowning silence for a moment before going out to the pigs. But she only said: 'Oh well, lucky nobody noticed it and got in.'

After breakfast Dido found the spare attic key and ran softly upstairs. She slipped the key into the keyhole – it fitted, the door opened; and she tiptoed on up the next flight. She found herself in a huge room with a sloping roof and low dormer windows. It stretched the length of the house and was filled with all sorts of odds and ends – old trunks, old boots, boxes, bales of sacking, flour-bags, two stuffed birds under a glass cover, some wooden stub-toe skates, an old fowling-gun, and so forth. Dido looked around sharply. She did not quite know what she was searching for, but almost at once she found it: faint, sandy footprints on the floor.

Those weren't made long ago, Dido said to herself. If they had been, they'd a soon dried up and blowed away.

A ship's ladder and a trapdoor led out on to the roof; looking down from the widow's-walk balcony Dido saw Penitence hanging cloths on the line. I'd best be getting back to work, she thought, before the old gal finds I'm up here, and she closed the trapdoor and tiptoed down the ladder. At its foot she stopped short, riveted by the sight of something that she had missed on her first hasty survey of the attic. Behind one of the chests, as if it had been hurriedly thrust out of sight, was a bundle of ladies' clothes: bonnet, gloves, a black silk dress and a cloak of grey twill. On top of the bundle was a pair of bottle-green boots.

Dido tiptoed over and inspected these. They had white stains on them.

Salt water, she said to herself. *Those* haven't been here long.

I'd best get outa here.

After giving another quick, darting look round the attic she slipped down the stairs and softly closed and locked the door behind her. None too soon, it seemed; she could hear terrified wails coming from Aunt Tribulation's room.

'Dido said I might go to bed!' Penitence was saying through her tears. 'Dido said we'd never find it in the dark. And indeed, Aunt Tribulation, we were dreadfully tired. Dido said th-that looking at night-time was a crazy notion.'

'She did, did she? She shall be punished for that. And you, miss, had better go out now, and I don't wish to see you again until the sheep is found! I am going to make myself obeyed from now on, do you understand?' Aunt Tribulation rapped on the floor with her stick.

Frowning, Dido walked into the room.

'So, girl!' Aunt Tribulation addressed her fiercely. 'You countermand my instructions, do you?'

'Yes,' Dido agreed. 'They was downright addlepated. And you didn't oughta shout at Pen that way, you'll scare her into historics. Pen,' she added, more in sorrow than anger, 'haven't I told you about not putting the blame on someone else? Stick up for yourself, girl!'

Pen gave her a miserable glance.

'Still, we mustn't be too hard on the old gal,' Dido added, with a sudden seraphic smile at Aunt Tribulation. 'When she shouts at you, Pen, remember her rheumaticks is hurting her cruel bad.'

Plainly Aunt Tribulation did not quite know how to deal with this.

'Penitence!' she snapped. 'Be off!'

Pen hesitated, then ran from the room.

'As for *you*,' Aunt Tribulation went on, 'you can miss your dinner. Go out, finish hoeing the potato field, then do the cornfield, and don't come back till it's finished.'

'Blister your potato field,' Dido replied calmly. 'I'm a-going to help Pen find that sheep. And if I miss my dinner, so will you, acos there won't be no one to bring it up to you.'

With which parting shot she ran downstairs to the kitchen. Pen had already started down the track. For several hours they searched unsuccessfully. There were plenty of sheep to be seen grazing the rough pasture as they went farther afield, but no one with the red C which was Captain Casket's mark. At last, when they were about halfway to Polpis and the sun was high in the sky, Dido suddenly cried: 'Oh, look, Pen! I do believe that there's a sheep with a red mark. Look, by the bushes. Quick, let's go arter him. Brrr! though; ain't it turned cold all of a sudden!'

While they were searching, the children had not noticed that a fine white sea-mist had come creeping over the island. Just as they started after the wandering sheep the mist caught up with and engulfed them.

'Hey, where are you, Pen?' Dido called anxiously.

'Here! I'm here!'

'Blame it, it's like walking through porridge! Where in thunderation is your voice coming from? Stand still, till I find you,' Dido said, feeling her way forward. But Pen suddenly shouted excitedly:

'Oh, I see it, I see the sheep! I believe I can catch it, too!'

There came the sound of running footsteps, which faded into the distance, then a disappointed cry, 'Oh, drat!'

Missed it, diagnosed Dido. Seconds later a damp, dew-spangled sheep bolted past her, nearly knocking her down, and disappeared into the dimness before she could grab it.

Blazes, Dido thought. Now I've lost 'em both, Pen *and* the sheep. Which'd I better go after? Pen, I reckon. The sheep can look after itself.

'Penitence!' she called lustily. 'Du-oo-tiful! Penitence! Where are you?'

No answer – only a plaintive, faraway bleat. Not *you*, woollyknob, Dido thought crossly. She floundered on into the smoky whiteness, tripping over wet, tangling shrubs, getting caught in thornbushes and low-growing holly, stumbling into holes and out of them again.

At last she struck a track which led uphill. Night was falling by now. Dispirited, weary, and very worried about Pen, she turned along it. Maybe I'll come to a house or a farm, she thought, where I can ask somebody to give me a hand hunting. At this rate the poor little brat stands a chance of being out all night and that'd just about *do* for Pen; she'd be seeing ghosts and boggarts for the rest of her life.

She hurried along the track, which sloped more and more steeply uphill and suddenly brought her out into a familiar barnyard. Why, curse it, Dido thought angrily, I'm *home*, what's the good o' that? No hopes Auntie Trib will give a hand. I'd best turn right round and go back the other way.

She was just turning wearily down the dusky track when a lantern light showed in the barn door.

'Dido!' called Pen's eager voice. 'Is that you?'

'Penny!' Dido exclaimed joyfully. 'You're back, then!'

'Yes, and, what do you think? I found the sheep again! Wasn't that a bit of luck? And, Dido, I have had such a curious adventure, listen – '

'You found the sheep? You brought it back all on your own?' Dido was amazed. 'I'd never a thought you had it in you, Pen! How ever did you manage to fetch it along? Where is it now?'

'In the barn. I led it,' Pen said.

'How, for gracious sakes?'

'Well,' Pen said rather shyly, 'I thought, how would Dido set about it? So as I hadn't got a rope I took off my

87

stockings and tied them together. It was the sheep that found the way home, not me. But I was dreadfully worried about where you'd got to, Dido. I'm ever so glad to see you.'

'Well, us'd better turn to and do the evening jobs while there's still a glim of daylight,' Dido said. 'You can tell me about your adventure when we're indoors making supper, Pen.'

They made haste with their tasks. Both were tired, wet, and hungry – though Dido grinned to herself as she thought how much hungrier Aunt Tribulation would be.

'Done the fowls? Good. That's the lot, then,' she said to Pen as they met at the back door.

'Oh, Dido,' breathed Pen fearfully. 'There's a light in the kitchen. Do you suppose – ?'

'Ssh!' Dido laid a finger on her lips and opened the kitchen door.

The kitchen was warm and bright but had lost some of its cheerful atmosphere. For Aunt Tribulation, fully dressed, was sitting in the rocking-chair by the stove. She was no less formidable up than she had been in bed; although she had taken off her tinted glasses the grey eyes they had concealed were cold and singularly unwelcoming. She wore a brown-and-white checked gingham dress, and a brown shawl; an enormous brown brooch with enough hair in it to stuff a pincushion fastened her white fichu. Her grey hair was strained back into a tight knot behind her head. She looked hungry.

'We found the sheep, Aunt Tribulation!' Pen announced proudly, after a momentary check in the doorway.

'So I should hope! You've taken long enough about it. Is the feeding done? Then hurry up and make my supper.'

'Pen must change first,' Dido said firmly. 'Her dress is sopping and she's got no stockings on.'

'Make haste, then. And, pray, why were the larder and

cellar doors locked, and what have you done with the keys?'

'Oh dear, did you want them?' Dido exclaimed innocently, drawing the keys out of her breeches pocket. 'I locked the doors acos we found the kitchen window open this morning and I was feared that burglars or wild animals might get in and steal our vittles or frighten you, Auntie Trib! O' course I never thought you'd be coming down for summat. I thought you was much too ill.'

Supper was taken in baleful silence and as soon as the children had washed up the dishes they escaped to bed, Dido almost bursting with suppressed laughter.

'Now tell me your adventures, Dutiful,' she said when they were snug under the quilt and the candle blown out.

'It was the strangest thing! After we lost each other I hunted for you, and I ran towards where I thought you had been standing, but I must have gone astray, for I ran on and on, a long way, and suddenly I found myself among high trees.'

'Trees? Why, there ain't but bushes and bits of scrub for miles.'

'I must have been in the Hidden Forest, you see,' Pen explained. 'It seemed so mysterious in the mist! When I called to you, as I had been doing on and off all the time, my voice echoed back so boomingly that I was afraid and dared not do it any more. I became confused in the wood and, trying to return the way I had come, went on, I think, in quite the wrong direction. Then all of a sudden I found myself up against a strange kind of barrier.'

'A fence, like?'

'No, not a fence, nor yet a wall . . . It was about as high as my head and very thick, and round like a great iron pipe; yes, like an iron pipe as big as a great tree-trunk.'

'That's rum,' Dido said. 'What held it up, then?'

'It was mounted all along its length – and it was *very* long, I never saw either end – on pairs of cartwheels.'

'Sounds as if maybe someone gets their water through it,' Dido suggested.

'But there are no farms anywhere near the Hidden Forest! And that's not the end of the story.'

'No? Hurry up, then, Dutiful, my eyes is closing in spite of themselves.'

'I thought I would feel my way along the pipe and so get out of the wood. But I had not gone very far when I bumped into a man.'

'What sort o' man? What was he doing?'

'Oh, Dido, he was strange! He was tapping on the pipe with a hammer. He gave a great start when I bumped into him – I would have screamed, but that *he* seemed even more frightened! I said I was lost, and which way to Soul's Hill? And he said, "Whisper", laying his finger on his lips and looking all round, and then he pointed which way I should go and led me to the edge of the wood. Then he whispered something, and it took me *such* a long time to make out what he was asking – he spoke in such a strange, foreign way! At last I realized that it was *boots* he wanted – he showed me his feet in thin, foreign-looking shoes, all wet and torn and muddy. So I promised I would see, there might be an old pair of Papa's sea-boots, and was that all he wanted? And he said – I *think* – that he had a great longing for something sweet, could I bring him any cakes or sugar or jam? To keep out the cold and damp. He said he would wait by the fork in the track every night from seven till nine.'

'Was he a beggar?'

'No indeed I am sure he was not! For he gave me money to pay for the boots – three English gold coins.'

'*English* coins? How d'you know they were English?'

'Because there is a picture of a king and the words *Carolus II Rex Br*.'

'Good cats alive!' Dido said. 'An old guinea piece! There's still quite a lot on 'em about, my pa used to get them for playing on his hoboy. D'you think the man was English, Pen?'

'He certainly was not American. But he didn't speak like you – his language was very queer. He was a sad-looking man with a face like a monkey, and big ears, and nearly bald. He said not to tell anyone that I had seen him, and if I came with the boots I was to croak like a night-heron. I *think* that was what he meant. And he said how glad he was that he would soon be back in Europe.'

'*Did* he?' Dido was more and more interested. If this man is really going back to Europe soon, she thought, and if I could make friends with him, and if I could get Pen fixed up somehow. . . . Who can the man be?

'We must look him out a pair o' boots tomorrow, Pen,' she said. 'I don't mind taking 'em to him if you're scared to go back. There's a deal of old boots up in the attic.'

And one pair of salt-stained, bottle-green ones that ought not to be there, she remembered, just before she went to sleep. Was it possible that Aunt Tribulation and the veiled stowaway of the *Sarah Casket* were one and the same person?

7

AUNT Tribulation had evidently decided that it was easier
to keep an eye on the girls if she got up, for the next day,
and all the days following, she was downstairs by seven
conducting a close scrutiny into all that went on. Indeed, as
Dido said, it was hard to believe that anything had ever
been the matter with her at all, so active and vigilant was
she now in pursuit of the children and in keeping them
hard at work.

'What does she take us for, perishing slaves?' grumbled
Dido.

It was by no means so easy to circumvent Aunt Tribulation now she had come downstairs. She was large and
strong, much larger than Dido, who remained small for her
age, though wiry and healthy. After Dido had been rapped
with a thimble numerous times, shut up in the grandfather
clock, deprived of meals, and made to sit on the whale's
jawbone for two hours, she saw that cunning and strategy
would be needed.

'As well as learning you to stand up to her, Pen, we've
someway got to make her *humble*, so she's real sorry for her
nasty nature and won't never bother you no more,' Dido
said one morning when they were out hoeing the cornfield.

'Do you think that would *ever* be possible?' sighed
Penitence.

'Have you written the letter to your Pa yet?'

'Yes, I have it in my chemise pocket.'

'Now, the mischief is, how're we going to get it to Nantucket to post it? No use to give it to old Mungo and ask *him* to take it to the mail office.'

Market days had come and gone, but Aunt Tribulation had sternly vetoed any idea that Dido or Pen might go in with the farm produce and do some shopping. Mungo, as usual, was sent on his own with a written list of groceries needed, which the owner of the main store would check and supply.

'If we could give the boots to your monkey-faced friend, *he* might post the letter for us,' Dido presently reflected. 'The trouble is how to wheedle Aunt Trib outa the house so's I can slip up to the attic and grab a pair. She never stirs except just into the yard.'

'I could tell her one of the sheep was sick and ask her to come up to the pasture.'

'She wouldn't care,' said Dido, who privately suspected that Aunt Tribulation knew little more about farming than the girls themselves. 'No, I have it, Penny, you must pretend you think I've fallen down the well. She wouldn't like that; no water, for one thing, and who'd do the work? She'd come out to help you grapple for me with a rope, and I could nip round to the back and climb up the willow tree and in our window.'

'But if she found out?' breathed Pen in horror.

'We could say you made a mistake. I'll drop my red shirt down, so's it looks like me down there,' said Dido. 'Pity we couldn't drop Auntie Trib herself down.'

In pursuit of this plan Dido contrived that evening to smuggle out her red shirt hidden in a pile of cheese-cloths, and dangle it down the well on a loop of thread until it caught on a projection about thirty feet below. The weather favoured them; it was misty again, and dusk was falling. Dido beckoned to Pen, who was in the hen-house, and whispered:

'Now, *screech*!'

'Oh,' faltered Pen, 'I don't believe I can!'

'Consarn it, Pen, you'd screech fast enough if a wild bull was rushing at you! Let on that one is!'

Pen gave a faint wail.

'Louder than that!' hissed Dido. 'Here, I'll do it!' She let out a fearful scream and then quickly slipped away round the corner of the house. The back door flew open and she heard Aunt Tribulation's voice.

'What's the matter?'

'Oh, Aunt T-Tribulation,' Pen stammered, 'I'm – I'm afraid Dido's in the well.'

'Blimey, *she'd* never get to Drury Lane,' Dido groaned to herself as she rapidly shinned up the willow tree. 'I never heard sich a rabbity bit of acting.' She scrambled in at their chamber window and pulled the spare attic key out of her pocket.

In a moment she had darted up to the attic and seized the largest and least worn pair of sea-boots; then, on a sudden thought, she tiptoed to the bundle of clothes behind the chest, pulled out a bonnet, and looked inside. It bore a London dressmaker's label and a name: Letitia M. Slighcarp. So did the cloak. Dido did not dare wait to examine the rest of the clothes; she fled silently down the stairs again, relocked the door, and was out and dropping from the willow tree all in the space of half a dozen heartbeats. She could still hear voices and splashings from the direction of the well so she thrust the boots into a clump of fern, strolled nonchalantly round the corner, and remarked:

'Hilloo? Dropped summat in the water?'

It was as well she arrived when she did for Aunt Tribulation had tied a rope round Pen, who had a perfectly ashen face and was shaking like a leaf, and was apparently on the point of lowering her to the assistance of her companion.

'You abominable girl! Where have you been?' Aunt Tribulation exclaimed, dashing at Dido and boxing her ears.

'Down the orchard, hanging up the cheese-cloths. Why, whatever's the matter?'

'Didn't you hear us shouting? Penitence thought you were in the well.'

'No, did she?' Dido replied, and burst out laughing. 'You *are* a one, Pen! You musta seen my shirt, that blew down when I was taking it to hang out. What a sell!' And she began to sing:

> 'Oh, what a sell,
> Dido's in the well.
> Who'll save her bacon?
> Auntie Tribulation!'

Aunt Tribulation, perfectly enraged, exclaimed, 'So you thought you'd make a fool of me, did you? Oh, you wicked little hussies, you shall have nothing but bread and water till the end of the week!' and she flew at Pen, who was the nearer, and shook her till she whimpered:

'It was Dido's idea, Aunt Tribulation, not mine! P-p-please stop! It was Dido's idea!'

'Oh-oh,' Dido said to herself. 'Here we go again. Now we *shall* be in the suds.'

But just at this critical moment an interruption occurred.

By now it was thick dusk and they could see only a few yards. Sounds, however, carried clearly in the mist, and they suddenly became aware of voices and footsteps approaching up the lane.

'Someone's coming!' breathed Penitence.

Aunt Tribulation turned her head sharply, heard the voices, and hissed, 'Go indoors, you girls! Make haste!'

Astonished, the girls did as they were bid, but went no farther than the deep porch. They were too curious to know who the visitors might be, for no callers had come to the farm since their arrival. Was Aunt Tribulation expecting somebody?

A voice – a boy's voice – said, 'Here we are, I b'lieve.

Ain't this the Casket place?' Then, apparently seeing Aunt Tribulation, 'Evening, ma'am. Would you be Miss Casket?'

'Yes I am,' she snapped, 'and I don't allow tramps and beggars on this land, so be off with you both!'

'But ma'am – ' the boy began to protest, and then Pen gasped as a man's voice said slowly and wonderingly:

'Why, isn't this Soul's Hill? We're home! However did we come to be here?'

'Be off!' Aunt Tribulation repeated.

'But ma'am! He's your brother! He's Cap'n Casket, don't you *know* him?' the boy blurted out and at the same moment Pen cried, '*Papa!* It's Papa come home!' and Dido shouted, 'Nate! Nate Pardon! What in mercy's name are you doing here?'

Both girls rushed forward joyfully, but checked a little as they came in view of Captain Casket. He looked thin and dazed, older than when they had seen him last; in a few weeks his hair seemed to have become a great deal greyer. But he smiled dreamily at Pen and said, 'Ah, Daughter, I am glad to see thee well.'

'Nate, what's happened?' Dido said quickly in a low tone. 'It's not the ship – the *Sarah Casket* – ?'

'We don't know,' Nate replied in the same tone. 'Let's get him indoors, shall we, before I tell you about it? He's still not himself.'

'Come in where it's warm and dry, Papa,' said Pen protectively, and took Captain Casket's hand to lead him in. He looked about him, still with the same bewildered expression, and said:

'So thee is living at home now, Penitence? I am glad of that. But who is this?' pointing to Dido.

'Why, Dido Twite, Papa. Don't you remember her?'

'Perhaps,' he said, passing a hand across his brow. 'I am tired. I become confused. Then who is looking after thee?'

'Papa, don't you remember Aunt Tribulation? Here she is! She has been – has been looking after us.'

'Ah yes, Sister Tribulation. She said she would come,' he murmured.

At this moment Aunt Tribulation, who had remained in the rear while these exchanges were going on, stepped forward, firmly took Captain Casket's other arm, and said:

'Well, Brother! Fancy seeing you home so soon! Deceived by the mist, and never thinking but that you were several thousand miles off, I almost took you for a tramp! This is a surprise, to be sure! What has become of your ship? Not a wreck, I trust?'

She seemed less than pleased at seeing her brother; indeed, thought Dido, she seemed decidedly put out.

Captain Casket looked at her in his wondering manner and murmured, 'Can it really be Sister Tribulation?'

'Of course it is I, Brother! Who else should it be?' she exclaimed impatiently, leading him in.

'Thee has aged – thee has aged amazingly.' He sat down in the rocker, shaking his head.

'We're none of us getting any younger!' snapped Aunt Tribulation.

'He is still a bit wandering in his wits, ma'am,' Nate explained in a low voice. 'What he's been through fair shook him up.'

'What happened?' Penitence inquired anxiously.

'It was the pink whale, you see.'

Nate glanced towards the captain, who seemed to have gone off into a dream, rocking back and forth, soothed by his chair's familiar creak and the homely things about him.

'We sighted her about ten days outa New Bedford,' Nate went on, 'and, my stars, did she lead us a dance! Round and round about, first north, then south, in the end we was nearer Nantucket than when we first started. At last we came right close to her, closer'n we'd ever been before; lots of the men hadn't rightly believed in her till then, but there she was, sure enough, just about like a great big strawberry ice. Well, Cap'n Casket, he says, "No man goes after her but me," he says, and he wouldn't let any o' the harpooners go in the boats. Just the one boat was lowered. He said I could be one of the rowers, because I had an eye for detail and a gift for language, and would be able to record the scene.'

'Well, and so? What happened?'

'She acted most uncommon,' Nate said. '*I* never see a whale carry on so. Soon's she laid eyes on Cap'n Casket she commenced finning and fluking and bellowing, she breached clean out of the water, she whistled, she dove down and broke up agin, she brung to dead ahead of us, facing us with her noddle end, and kind of *smiled* at the cap'n, then she lobtailed with her flukes as if – as if she was wagging her tail like a pup, she rolled and she rounded, she thrashed and tossed her head like a colt, she acted justabout like a crazy dolphin. By and by she settled and started in swimming to and forth under the boat, rubbing her hump on the keel, and that busted the boat right in half.'

'She didn't know her own strength,' murmured Captain Casket as if to himself. 'She meant no harm. It was only in play.'

'What happened then?' breathed Dido, round-eyed.

'I don't know what happened to the other rowers in the boat,' Nate said. 'We was all tossed out a considerable way. I just about hope they got picked up by the ship. I was swimming near Cap'n Casket in the water when we was both heaved up as if a volcano had busted out under us, and blest if it wasn't old Rosie hoisting us up on her back! And you'll never believe it, but she started to run, then, and she never stopped till she brung to and dumped us off Sankaty beach. Then she sounded and we never saw her no more. So we waded ashore and walked here – I reckon the cap'n had best be put to bed, ma'am.'

Indeed Pen, who found this tale almost too frightening

to contemplate, had already busied herself with heating some bricks in the oven for the captain's bed, and warming one of his spare nightshirts before the fire.

'Oh, Papa,' she paused by him to say, 'I am so *thankful* you were spared.'

He patted her head absently. 'Is that thee, Daughter? What is thee doing on board? I thought I left thee in New Bedford.'

'He must certainly go to bed,' pronounced Aunt Tribulation.

'I'll be off home, ma'am, now I've seen him safe here,' Nate said. 'My folks live over to Polpis.'

'But have a bite to eat first – have a hot drink!' Dido exclaimed. 'Try some o' Pen's herb tea and her pumpkin pie – it's first-rate. And you haven't told us what happened to the ship – did they see you thrown into the sea and picked up by the pink 'un?'

'I guess not,' Nate said. 'There was considerable fog come up. Like as not if the other men gets picked up, they'll reckon me and Cap'n Casket musta been drowned.'

'Well you ain't, that's the main thing,' Dido said. 'Oh, Nate, your bird! Poor Mr Jenkins! Was he with you in the boat?'

'No, no, chick, he'll be all right,' Nate said, laughing. 'Reckon Uncle 'Lije'll look after him for me till they puts back into port.'

Aunt Tribulation now bustled Captain Casket upstairs while Pen started heating a posset for him. 'Oh, Dido!' she whispered. 'I'm so happy Papa has come home! For Aunt Tribulation will hardly – will hardly like to be so unkind to us while he is here.'

Dido nodded sympathetically. In fact she was by no means so easy in her mind about the situation. For a moment at first she had hoped that, if Aunt Tribulation really was an imposter, she would be exposed by Captain Casket's failure to recognize her as his sister, but it was soon plain that he was too wandering in his wits for this to be likely. And if he continued so, Dido feared that he would have small effect on Aunt Tribulation's sharp and bullying ways. And what would become of his promise to secure Dido a passage to England? In any case she could hardly go off and leave Pen while matters were in such a train. Her heart sank. There seemed less and less chance of her ever reaching home again.

Nate wiped his mouth and rose. 'Thanks for the pie, it was real good,' he said. 'I'll be on my way.'

'Oh, Nate,' Pen said earnestly, 'I'm so *grateful* to you for bringing Papa safe home!'

It was the first time she had ever plucked up courage to address him directly, and Dido gave her an approving look. Nate smiled down at her.

'That's all right, little 'un,' he answered awkwardly. 'Hope he's soon better.'

'I'll come out with you,' Dido said. 'I hain't shut up the hens yet.' And she muttered to Pen, 'I'll take the boots along to you-know-who while I'm out. If *she* asks where I am, say the black sow got loose and I'm chasing her. Needn't bother about getting your letter posted now, that's one thing.'

'Nor we need!' Pen said, recollecting. 'Oh, Dido, take the poor man this sassefras candy too!'

'I'm coming a piece of the way with you,' Dido explained to Nate when they were outside. 'I've an errand in the forest. Lucky there's a moon behind the clouds.'

The sandy track showed up white ahead of them.

'The forest?' Nate said, surprised. 'That's a mighty queer place to have an errand.'

'Oh, Nate!' Dido exclaimed. '*Everything's* queer altogether! I'm right down glad to see you, I don't mind saying. I reckon there's some regular havey-cavey business going on.'

'What sort o' business?'

'Well,' Dido said, 'I don't reckon as how things can be wuss'n they are now, so I might as well tell you the whole story.'

Which she proceeded to do, omitting nothing: the veiled lady on the ship, Mr Slighcarp and the boots, the torn-up letter, the night departure in New Bedford harbour, the mysterious visitor at the farm who had so inexplicably vanished, the footprints in the attic, the sounds in the night and the open window, and the green boots and clothes marked Letitia Slighcarp.

'Whatever do you make of it all?' she asked.

'Seems as if old Slighcarp's muxed up in it somehow, dunnit?' Nate said. 'He never sailed this trip, so he must be ashore somewhere.'

'Yes, I know. Do you suppose he's maybe lurking in these parts? But then who's *she*, if she's not Aunt Tribulation? And where's the real Aunt Tribulation? Oh, Nate, d'you think they could have *murdered* her?'

'Easy now,' said Nate. 'One thing at a time. You say there was a letter at Galapagos saying Auntie Trib could come to Nantucket. Maybe there was another letter, written later, saying she'd changed her mind. Maybe Mr Slighcarp read that one and tore it up.'

'Yes, but why?'

'Why, you chucklehead, so's he could put the stowaway lady in Aunt Trib's place. She must be some kin of his, his wife or sister.'

'The second letter had sprung open with the damp, I remember now,' Dido said. 'That could be it. Croopus, Nate, ain't you clever! She must be Letitia M. Slighcarp, and old foxy-face is skulking somewheres round about, coming to see her when we're outa the way.' She chuckled. 'He musta got locked in that night when I put the keys under my pillow, and had to climb out the window. He musta been in the house the whole time. No wonder the old gal wasn't over-and-above pleased to see Cap'n Casket come home! No wonder she thought he was a tramp at fust! She'd never met him before. Mr Slighcarp musta brought her here while we was still in New Bedford with Cousin Ann. But what's the point o' lodging her here? Someone'd be sure to rumble her in the end.'

'It surely is a puzzle,' Nate said. 'But wait a minute, wait! Old Slighcarp had to leave England and skedaddle abroad in a hurry because he'd been plotting against the king, and the militia was after him. Maybe it's the same with her. Maybe she had to skip quick, and when he saw this chance he grabbed it. We was several days off the English coast. That would explain why old man Slighcarp was so powerful keen to follow the pink whale round thataway, if he knew Miss Slighcarp wanted picking up.'

'Of course! That must be it! But what'll us do now?'

'Well,' Nate said, 'I s'pose the best would be to get holt o' the real Aunt Tribulation. But you still haven't told me why you're going to the forest.'

'That's summat quite different. Pen met a rummy little cove there, camping beside a big iron pipe, and he asked her to get him some boots and candy. He gave her three English guineas and said he was soon going back to Europe. I was curious about him; I reckoned I'd go along to see was there a chance of my getting a berth on his ship. Reckon this changes things, though; I can't lope off till it's settled about Auntie Trib.' She gave a deep sigh.

'It seems to me,' Nate said, 'as how this man must be connected with old Slighcarp. Else what is he doing, camped in the middle o' Nantucket?'

'Maybe so. Pen said he was scared stiff o' summat. He told her to whisper, and to croak like a night-heron when she came to meet him.' Dido chuckled at the thought of Pen trying to imitate a night-heron. 'Maybe he's scared of old Slighcarp?'

'I dunno what to make of it,' said Nate. 'Hadn't I better

stay with you while you give him the boots? Sounds a mite chancy to me.'

'Done,' said Dido promptly. 'Maybe you'll be able to smoke his lay. But you better glide along kind of cagey in case he sheers off when he sees there's two of us.'

'Where was you meeting him?'

'At the fork in the track.'

'That's only half a mile now.' Nate sank his voice to a whisper. 'You keep on the track and I'll slide alongside in the brishes.'

Dido nodded. He slipped into shelter and she went on at a good pace, but walking as silently as she could on the sandy path.

When she reached the fork, easily visible in the cloud-filtered moonlight, she squatted down by a wild plum thicket, cupped her hands round her mouth, and let out a gentle croak. This was answered almost at once, and somebody moved out of the thicket. It was not possible to see him very clearly, but Dido recognized the small, bald man of Pen's description.

'Is it little kindgirl?' he whispered. 'You boots with?'

'Yus,' Dido whispered back. 'I brung 'em.'

'But you are unsame child!' Alarm and suspicion could be heard in his voice.

'I'm her friend, guvnor,' Dido reassured him. 'She was a-seeing to her pa and couldn't come out. Sorry we ain't been before – it warn't so easy to get aholt o' the boots. This here's candy.'

'Ah, miracle, nobleness! All the time is only to eat fish, fish, fish! You are a heaven-sentness,' he whispered. His language was both guttural and hissing; Dido found it very hard to follow. He was already sitting in a bayberry bush and pulling on the boots with little grunts of satisfaction. 'Gumskruttz! Forvandel! Zey are of a fittingness! I am all obligation.'

He fervently kissed Dido's hand, much to her astonishment, dropped his old shoes in the bush, then, whispering, 'Plotslakk! Momentness – I bring you – ' vanished back into the thicket. Almost at once he reappeared, thrust a prickly, wriggling bundle into Dido's arms, tried to kiss her hand again, thought better of it, said urgently, 'Each nat will be a bringness. Hommens. For you. If you bring kaken?'

'Kaken?'

'Pankaken. Appelskaken. Siggerkaken.'

'Cakes,' Dido guessed. 'I'll try,' she whispered.

'Is good, noblechild! Wunderboots! Blisscandy! I say good nat.'

Before she could stop him, he faded into the bush as if something had startled him. 'Hey!' Dido whispered as loud as she dared. 'Mister! Come back!'

But he was gone.

After a few moments Nate rose soundlessly out of the shrubs where he had been lying, almost at Dido's feet.

'Well,' she whispered. 'What did you make of *that* lot? And what in tarnation's he given me?'

'Lobsters.' Nate identified the wriggling mass. 'Big 'uns too. He was a rum job, wasn't he?'

'One thing's for certain – ' Dido was disappointed – 'he ain't English. Pen was right. Dear knows what peg-legged lingo that was he spoke.'

'I'd sure like to know what he's doing in Nantucket,' Nate muttered. 'Up to no good, I bet. I've a good mind to nip into the forest and scout around.'

'Oh, yes, Nate, let's!'

'Not you, chick. It wants smart scout-work. One's enough.'

'I can snibble along jist as quiet as you!' Dido said, hurt. They argued about it in whispers; Dido was so insistent on coming that in the end Nate was obliged to give way.

Proceeding with the utmost caution they crept towards

the forest. The ground began to slope steeply downhill and presently they were in the shelter of the trees where, as it was much darker, they had to go forward very slowly, one step at a time.

Nate, who was a couple of paces ahead, suddenly let out a stifled grunt.

'What's up?' breathed Dido, coming alongside.

'Nearly busted my nose on the tarnal thing. Must be the pipe,' he muttered. 'We'd best follow it.'

They turned at right angles and stole along beside the pipe, slowly and carefully, Nate still in the lead. Presently he paused. A faint light showed ahead and voices could be heard. Dido moved up as close behind Nate as she could and peered past him. The lobsters which she still carried nipped the hand that Nate had put out to check her and he let out a hiss of protest.

'Mind, stoopid!'

'Sorry!'

They could dimly see a small log hut. A fire burnt in front of it and three or four men were gathered round talking in low voices.

'Where's the old professor gone?' one of them said.

'Oh, he likes to mooch about the wood on his own in the evening. He's everlastingly on the lookout for the black-crowned night-heron or some sich foolishness. He's all right, don't fret about him, he won't go far.'

'I'd rather he stayed in camp, just the same.'

With a start, Dido recognized this voice as Mr Sligh-carp's. She gave Nate's shin a gentle kick. He nodded.

'When's the *Dark Diamond* due?' another voice asked.

'Any day now.'

'Thank the lord. I can justabout do with a decent smoke. I'm *cheesed-off* with smoking peat and eating shellfish. Will the ship wait and take us off at the same time's she leaves the charge and shot?'

'Depends on how the professor makes out. If he can finish before she gets here, fine; we can blast off and then clear out.'

'What about your sister?'

'Take her too, o' course.'

'But ain't she *wanted* over there?'

'Well, so are most of us wanted, aren't we?' Mr Sligh-carp said impatiently. 'But don't you see, things'll be different in England by the time we get back?'

'Oh, ah, so they will. O' course. I'd forgot. But, say, how'll we *know*? Suppos'n old Breadno makes a mistake? We don't want to go sailing over and put our heads into a hank-noose and end up on Tyburn!'

'We'll sail to Hanover first, dunderhead! The news will have reached them by then.'

'Aye, that would be best,' the other voice agreed gloomily. 'I does so *long* to get my chops round a bit o' British bubble-and-squeak.'

'Bubble-and-squeak! It'll be roast goose and champagne when you get it, cully!'

'I'm going to look for the professor,' Mr Slighcarp said uneasily. He rose to his feet.

At this moment one of the lobsters Dido carried, which

had been squirming more and more vigorously, escaped from her grip and fell into a bush. She grabbed it.

'Hark! What was that?' Mr Slighcarp said, turning sharply.

'It's only the professor, guvnor, here he comes.'

By a great piece of good fortune the man to whom Dido had given the boots – apparently the professor referred to – stepped into the clearing at this moment.

'Hey there, Professor Breadno, see some good night birds?'

'We're all justabout night birds if you ask me,' yawned one of the men. 'I'm going to turn in.'

Dido kicked at Nate's shin again and began to step delicately backwards. She was apprehensive of another accident with the lobsters. Nate waited for a few more minutes before following, but presently joined her on the edge of the forest.

'Did you hear any more?' she breathed.

'Nope. They were asking the prof where he got his boots and he said he found 'em in a bog.'

'I wonder if they'll believe him. What a parcel of peevy coves, eh? Regular mill-kens.'

'I still can't make out what they're at,' Nate said, as they hurried silently back to the path. 'They seem to be Hanoverians, that's plain, but what the mischief are they doing in Nantucket? We ain't got none o' your fancy kings over here, a plain president's good enough for us.'

'It's plumb mysterious,' Dido agreed. 'Tell you what, though, I'll take the little professor cove some cakes – if I can slip past old Mortification – and try to get a bit more outa him. Supposin' I can make out what he means.'

'I'm glad I came back home,' Nate said. 'I think it's downright rusty the way these lowdown deadbeats make themselves at home in our island, and whatever deviltry they're plotting, I think they ought to be rousted out someway.'

'I'm agreeable,' Dido said. 'Specially if Aunt Tribulation's one of 'em. I allus thought she was a no-good. What d'you think we ought to do, Nate?'

'I'll think, and let you know. I'll stay home for a piece, anyhow. My Ma'll be quite glad to have me minding the sheep and helping with the chores. I won't try to get another ship till the *Sarah Casket* comes back. I'd sooner ship with Cap'n Casket, when he's better, I'm used to him.'

'If he *gets* better,' Dido said doubtfully. 'If he don't I reckon I'm stuck here for life.'

'Well there's plenty wuss places than Nantucket you could be stuck in.'

As they were by now a good way from the forest, Nate burst into song:

'I'll tend to my lambkins in pasture and grove
A shepherd I'll be and daylong will I rove;
In the isle of Nantucket I'll finish my days
A-following my sheep and a-watching them graze.'

'I do wonder what those scallions is up to,' Dido speculated.

'Well, whatever it is, it's bad business. I'll tell you one thing, chick.'

'What's that?'

'That there pipe of Pen's ain't no pipe but a *gun* – and it's the longest gun I ever laid eyes on!'

'Croopus!' said Dido. 'That's why the ship's coming with powder and shot. But who're they going to shoot, d'you reckon?'

'Search me. But whoever it is, they've gotter be stopped.'

8

*Captain Casket's illness – Dido sees the doctor –
the professor in the bog – an abominable plot –
Aunt Tribulation overhears*

To Dido's surprise and concern there were still lights
burning in the farm as she approached. Surely it was long
past the usual hour for bedtime? Did this mean that
Aunt Tribulation had seen through Pen's story of the
straying sow and was waiting up to conduct an inquiry?
Prudently, she hid the pair of lobsters in a bush lest they
should lead to questions.

When Dido walked into the kitchen, however, she
saw at once that the unusual wakefulness was not on
her account. The stove was roaring, a large black
kettle steamed, Pen was anxiously heating a poultice,
while Aunt Tribulation, with a grim expression, aired
blankets, nightcaps, and chest-protectors before the
fire.

'Oh, Dido!' Pen exclaimed. 'Papa is dreadfully unwell,
he is in a fever! I have tried him with everything, balsam
and cordial and rheumatic pills, but none of them did him
any good. He tosses and turns so, and throws off the
bedclothes; he seems to think he is in a boat.'

'Did you find the sow, miss?' Aunt Tribulation snapped
at Dido.

'She's in the barn,' Dido replied. 'D'you think we
should get a doctor?' she said to Pen.

'Oh, I do! Would you go for one, Dido?'

'A doctor will hardly thank you for fetching him out at
this hour,' Aunt Tribulation remarked sourly. 'Here,
child, take these warm things up to your father, *I'm* going

to bed. I've done all that can be expected in my delicate state of health.'

'Isn't she perfectly hateful,' Pen whispered when Aunt Tribulation had departed. 'She doesn't seem to care a *bit* about poor Papa. As for her "delicate state of health" I don't believe there was ever a thing wrong with her.' Pen was distractedly looking through the store cupboard in search of more remedies. 'What's in this jar? Can you read the label, Dido? It's dear Mamma's tiniest writing. I can't make it out.' Impatiently she rubbed the tears from her eyes. 'Oh, Dido, supposing Papa were to *die*?'

'We shan't suppose any such nonsense,' Dido said firmly. 'Huckleberries in gin, this is, smells like stingo stuff. Try them on him, Penny, see if he likes 'em.'

They hurried upstairs with the warm clothes and the poultice, the pot of huckleberries, and a stone jar full of boiling water for the captain's feet.

It was very difficult to get him wrapped up and poulticed. As Pen had said, he kept throwing himself about, crying, 'Towno! Towno! Alow from aloft! I'm all beset, bring to! Give it to her, she's pitching. Her spiracle's under . . . Stern all, we're stove!'

He sprang up in bed, and the poultice flew across the room.

'Never mind the dratted poultice,' Dido said at last in exasperation. 'It's all cold and dusty by now anyways. Here, you hold his hands a moment while I try to slip some o' these huckleberries down him. Hold tight!'

Pen held on manfully. 'Papa! Don't you know me?' she pleaded. 'It's Penitence!'

'Thar she blows!' shouted Captain Casket. But as he kept his mouth open to prolong the bellow, Dido neatly popped in a spoonful of the huckleberries. The captain immediately shut his mouth. He swallowed. A surprised expression came over his face.

'Quick! Another spoonful!' whispered Pen.

When Dido raised the spoon again he opened his mouth
eagerly, and she was able to feed him the rest of the potful
without difficulty. He murmured to himself, 'Truly it has
been a wonderful summer for the fruit, wonderful! We
must all –'

His eyelids fluttered down and he suddenly fell back on
the pillow, fast asleep.

'*That's* a mussy,' Dido said. 'Now let's snug him up
warm and then as soon as it's light, Pen, I'll go for the
doctor. D'you know his name?'

'No, but anyone in Nantucket town would be able to tell
you.'

They wedged the captain about with hot bottles and laid
several comforters on him. Pen sat down by him, anxiously
holding his hand. Since her father had come home, needing
her help, Pen was a changed creature. She seemed to have
thrown aside her needless fears and become quite practical
and self-reliant. But just the same, Dido could see that this
was no time to burden her with the tale of the conspirators
in the wood; Captain Casket's illness was enough to worry
about.

It did not seem worth trying to sleep as there wanted but

an hour to daylight; instead Dido fed the animals and harnessed Mungo to the cart.

'I'm off, now, Dutiful,' she called softly up the stairs. 'I'll be as quick as I can.'

Jumping into the cart, she shook up the reins, and started Mungo at a rattling pace towards Nantucket town. One thing, she thought, it's nice to get away from Auntie Trib for a bit. I hope she don't give poor Pen the runaround while I'm gone; likely she'll sleep a good while yet as she was up so late.

The day was a fine one and her spirits rose. Dawn had flooded the upland commons with ruddy light and crimsoned the distant line of the sea. Old Rosie would look just the thing out there now, Dido said to herself. For the first time she recalled Nate's strange tale of how the pink whale had seemed to welcome Captain Casket. A rummy business altogether, Dido reflected. Sounded as if old Rosie had taken a fancy to him somewhere and remembered him, but why? He wasn't so handsome, why should she go out of her way to put down the red carpet for him?

Mungo was suffering from several days' lack of exercise and bolted along so fast that when they descended the gentle incline into Nantucket town it was still quite early. Not many people were about in the cobbled streets. Dido bore right towards the waterfront and left Mungo tethered to a post in Whale Street while she asked her way on foot.

'Old Doc Mayhew?' said a fisherman on the wharf. 'He lives on Orange Street. That ain't but a few minutes from here.'

The doctor lived in a handsome white house, Quaker style, with a fanlight and three windows on each floor. Dido banged loudly on the door and told the housekeeper that Doctor Mayhew was wanted urgently.

'He ain't taken but a mouthful of breakfast. Could you wait ten minutes?'

'Oh well, I guess Cap'n Casket won't die in that time,'

Dido agreed. She was dying for some breakfast herself and strolled back, looking for a baker's shop, but was soon startled by a familiar voice, calling in the next street:

'In the spring of the year when the blood is too thick
There is nothing so good as a sassefras stick!
    Who'll buy my stick candy
    So nice and so dandy?
Pickled limes, jelly doughnuts, come snap 'em up
    quick!'

'Nate!' Dido exclaimed, and ran into Main Street, where she found Nate making his way slowly along in a small pony cart laden with trays of delicacies, presumably made by Mrs Pardon.

'Hallo, chick!' he said when he saw her, and then filled his lungs again and shouted:

'I've several different kinds
    Of pickled tamarinds!
Try my pickled bananas, walk up, take your pick!
Try my liquorice roots, worth a dollar a lick!'

A number of housewives came to their doors and bought his wares, which included doughnuts, biscuits and waffles.

'Try my
  lemony
    wintergreen
      sassefras
        peppermint
superfine candy, a penny a stick!'

Children came running for the dazzlingly coloured candy sticks.

He called:

'Popcorn and peanuts and pecans and popovers
Wintergreen wafers and hermits and jumbles
Gingersnaps, crullers, marshmallows and turnovers
Sample a cookie and see how it crumbles!'

Dido bought some popovers and found them delicious.

'Nate, have you thought what we oughta do yet?' she asked, when there was a momentary lull in the stream of customers.

'Yes,' he said, glancing about. 'I've thought. We must tell the Mayor. Likely he won't be so keen to have a mess o' Hanoverian English plotting on his island.'

'That sounds like sense. What's the Mayor's name, where does he live?'

'It's old Doc Mayhew, he lives on Orange Street.'

'Why,' Dido exclaimed, 'I'm jist a-going to fetch him to come and see Cap'n Casket who's got the raving fevers. Couldn't be more handy! I'll tell him the whole tale as we drive home. See you later, Nate.'

Doctor Mayhew was a fine-looking old gentleman with white hair and a frill of white whiskers all round his red face, so that he looked rather like an ox-eyed daisy. He wore a green coat with brass buttons as big as penny-pieces, and a snowy-white ruffled shirt.

'Hallo!' he said at sight of Dido. '*You're* a young 'un I've never laid eyes on before. Didn't bring *you* into the world! Living out at the Casket place, are ye?'

'That's it,' Dido agreed. 'I'm staying there, keeping young Pen Casket company till she's gotten used to her Auntie Tribulation.'

'Tribulation Casket? Has *she* come back to live on the island? Why, I haven't set eyes on her since she was a young thing of fifteen. She went off to live with her grandmother, then, in Vine Rapids.'

'Oh,' Dido was disappointed. 'Guess you'll find she's changed a bit, then.'

'Lively young gal she used to be,' the doctor said reminiscently. 'Always one for a song or a bit of dancing or horse-back riding.'

'Croopus,' said Dido. 'She ain't like that now. Doc Mayhew, can I ask you summat?'

'Why, certainly, my child! How can I help you?'

'Well, you see, it's like this, Doc. There's a whole passel of Hanoverian plotters on Nantucket and we think Miss Casket is one of 'em.'

'Hanoverians?' Doctor Mayhew seemed somewhat bewildered.

'Yes, sir. English Hanoverians. They're all a-plotting against the English king.'

Doctor Mayhew laughed heartily. 'Why, child, what an imagination you have!'

'It's true,' Dido said indignantly. 'I ain't bamming you!'

'Why, child, even if you were right, what harm could they do the English king over here? This sounds like pure fancifulness to me.'

'They've got a gun,' Dido said stubbornly. 'They're all a-camping in the Hidden Forest, except for Miss Casket that is, and they've got a mighty great gun about a mile long.'

'Oh no, my child. I have heard of those men. They are scientists, and that is not a gun but a telescope; quite a natural mistake to make. I believe they are ornithologists, studying our bird-life; somebody said they wished to see a black-crowned night-heron. English ornithologists, that's all they are.'

'Orny thologists be blowed,' said Dido. 'Ornery jail-birds is what they are, and they're here to do some piece of sculduggery; we heard 'em plotting it the other night in the wood; then they'll go back to England in their ship the *Dark Diamond*.'

'That's all right, then,' said Doctor Mayhew comfortably. 'And good riddance to 'em, whether jailbirds or bird fanciers. We've got no call to worry our heads about a pack of foreign English, even if they do put in a bit o' plotting in the evenings after they've finished bird-watching for the day. This is a free country, dearie. And we keep ourselves to ourselves on Nantucket, we've no truck with such highfalutin' nonsense as kings; even the president don't bother us much. Live and let live is our motto. And as for Miss Tribulation getting mixed up in such doings, that sounds like moonshine to me.'

'Maybe it does,' Dido said crossly, 'but it's true jist the same. You see she ain't Miss Tribulation. She's only pretending to be her.'

'Who the blazes,' said Doctor Mayhew, 'would want to *pretend* to be Miss Tribulation Casket? You've been reading too many fairy-tales, that's what's the matter with you! Now, you tell me what ails Cap'n Casket?'

Deciding that Nate might be a better hand at convincing the doctor, Dido abandoned the subject of the Hanoverians and described Captain Casket's symptoms and strange delirious remarks. Doctor Mayhew was very interested in the tale of the pink whale.

'Is that so?' he kept saying. 'That's mighty interesting. And why shouldn't there be a pink whale now? There's a-plenty pink fish, pink pearls, pink shells, pink seaweed in the ocean – why not a pink whale?'

'And why did she carry on so when she saw Cap'n Casket?'

'Oh, that's simple enough. Guess she was the little pink whale-calf he put back in the sea when he was a boy; he told me that tale once: he found her beached and dragged her back in. *And* of course, whales being warm-blooded, warm-hearted, long-lived critters – I've heerd of 'em living to a century or more – she'd naturally remember him kindly. They're kin to dolphins, ye know, and dolphins are right sympathetic to the human race.'

'Oh, I see,' Dido said. 'Kind of old childhood pals, like? Well, we'll be properly in the basket if he wants her to sit by his bed and hold his hand. Let's hope he's a bit better time we get back.'

Captain Casket did not seem to be much better, though, when they arrived at Soul's Hill. He was wild and feverish, rolled about in his bed, and kept throwing imaginary harpoons at unseen whales.

'He needs a dose of poppy syrup,' Doctor Mayhew said. 'That'll give him some rest.'

He administered a draught. Immediately Captain Casket fell back as if he had been pole-axed and began snoring loudly.

'That'll fix him for a good few hours,' Doctor Mayhew said with satisfaction. 'Powerful strong it is, the way I mix it. Here' – to Pen – 'I'll leave ye the bottle, but don't give him any more unless I'm delayed getting back to ye and he seems worse. Now, why don't I drive your mule on to Polpis, where I've another patient, and bring him back tomorrow, that'll save you an extra trip to Nantucket?'

Aunt Tribulation came into the room.

'Well, Tribulation,' the doctor said, 'I'd not have known ye, but I suppose we're all getting a bit long in the tooth. Remember when I pushed you in the creek and you were so mad at me?'

'Yes I do,' said Aunt Tribulation frostily. 'And it's not a thing to boast about. It was not the act of a gentleman!'

Doctor Mayhew laughed very heartily at this and took his leave, pinching Pen's cheek. As soon as the door closed behind him, Aunt Tribulation went off to her room for a nap.

The girls sat with Captain Casket through the afternoon, but he continued to sleep peacefully and never stirred. During this time Dido took the opportunity of telling Pen part of what had happened in the forest, and the conclusions that she and Nate had reached. But she did not mention their suspicions of Aunt Tribulation; she thought the news that Miss Casket might be a female English ex-convict would prove too much for Pen's new-found courage.

At last, when dusk was beginning to fall, Dido said,

'Maybe us'd better get the jobs done while Cap'n Casket's still quiet.'

Pen agreed that it would be safe to leave her father for a while.

As they were feeding the pigs Pen thought she heard cries from the bottom pasture.

'Dido, quick!' she cried, looking over the fence. 'There's somebody in trouble down there on the bog!'

At the foot of the hill was a small cranberry bog which had been neglected until it was half grown over with bushes and straggly trees. They could hear the cries for help clearly now, and see somebody floundering about among the crimson hummocks.

'I'll go,' Dido said, grabbing a long-handled wooden hayrake. 'You'd best stay here, Pen, in case your pa wakes.'

She bolted down the hill, calling, 'Hold on, I'm a-coming!'

When she reached the edge of the bog she saw that the person in distress was the little Professor Breadno. He was mired up to his knees, completely stuck; his eyes were bulging with fright and his ears stood out like wings.

'Well you *are* a clodpole, ain't you?' Dido said. 'How ever did you come to get into sich a pickle?'

'Is hoping seeing bird, seeing nat-herrn,' he explained humbly.

Dido crawled out with caution on to a fairly safe-looking hummock and extended the rake in his direction. He was just able to grab it.

'That's the dandy! Hold on between the spikes!' Dido said, demonstrating. 'Now I'm a-going to pull, so when I say heave, you shove off like an old bullfrog. Ready? – *Heave!*'

She threw herself back, pulling until every muscle in her skinny frame seemed about to snap. The professor came out of the mud a reluctant six inches, and fell forward on to his knees.

'Keep a-going, don't stop now, don't sink!' shouted Dido, throwing herself back again. 'Heave some more, come on, put a bit o' gumption into it. Don't pull *me* in!'

She dragged him slowly through the mud.

'If you've lost those boots I shan't half give you whatfor,' she added. 'We've had trouble enough over them already.' He was so muddy that it was impossible to tell whether he had them on or not.

'Skrek verlige öfalt!' he exclaimed, looking at himself dolefully, and then, politely, to Dido, 'Is a much nick of time, treasurechild!'

'Yes, thanks, but don't kiss my hand again,' she said, retreating with haste. 'You better come up and get under the pump. Hope Auntie Trib's still asleep.' She beckoned him and he followed trustfully, dripping mud and ooze at every step.

'Mercy!' exclaimed Pen at sight of him. 'I'll put on a kettle.'

'Pump first,' Dido said grimly. 'It's *us* as'll have to scrub the kitchen floor if he walks on it in that state. Make him some o' your herb tea, Penny.'

The poor little man submitted meekly to being pumped over; 'I sank you; sank you!' he kept repeating piteously.

'I should jistabout think you nearly did sink me! Guess you're clean enough now, you can go into the kitchen. Don't make a noise.' She gestured towards the door where Pen had an old suit of Captain Casket's ready. It was far too big for the professor and they had to kilt it up here and there with lengths of string.

He drank the herb tea with loud expressions of appreciation; they gathered it was something he had not expected to find outside his native land.

'Hjavallherbteegot! Wundernice! Gratefulness!'

'That's all right,' Dido said. 'Have some gingerbread. Now we don't want to get you into trouble with your friends, but we do want you to tell us about that gun o' yours, professor.'

'Gun?'

'Cannon. Pistol. Bang, bang!'

'Aha, königsbang! Is soon blowing up London.'

'*What?*'

'Is will be monstershoot, grosseboom, across –'

He looked about the room and saw an old, silvery globe of the world on one of the dresser shelves. With a finger he traced a course on it from the island of Nantucket up over Nova Scotia across the north Atlantic to London. 'Is shooting up palast – Sint Jims Palast, not?'

'Shooting right across the Atlantic? Blowing up St James's Palace. Is that what he means, Pen?'

'Goodso!' the professor said, delighted. 'Is fine shoot, not? And is all mine, Doktor Axeltree Breadno, mine mattematic kalkulätted!'

'But, Professor, blowing up London!'

'London – not. Sönmal Kungspalast.'

'Only the king's palace,' Dido guessed. He nodded. 'Croopus, that's mighty pretty aiming, I must say. But, honestly, Professor, you mustn't blow up the poor old king, must he, Pen? What harm's he ever done to you?'

'No indeed, it would be very wrong,' Penitence agreed.

But they seemed unable to convey this idea to the professor. 'Is cleverness, not?' he kept saying. 'Will being magnifibang!' He was so pleased with his amazing feat of having made a gun that would shoot right across the Atlantic and hit St James's Palace that he could not see any wrong in it.

'He's looking forward to the bang,' Dido said exasperatedly.

'Is being donderboom!' he agreed with an eager nod.

'And will pushing – lookso – ' He made a gesture on the globe with his finger, from Nantucket to the New Jersey coast. It took them some time to see what he meant.

'You mean,' said Dido at last, 'that the what-d'you-call-'em – the recoil from the shot – will push Nantucket right back against that place, Atlantic City?'

'Is so!' he said in triumph. 'Is byggdegrit, not?'

'It certainly is! Just wait till the Mayor hears this! It ought to change his notions about not interfering. "We keep ourselves to ourselves on Nantucket," he said.' Dido couldn't help bursting into a fit of laughter. Then she sobered up. Pen was looking absolutely aghast.

'Push Nantucket all that way? But the houses would fall down!'

'That wouldn't be the half of it, I dessay,' Dido said. 'Think of the waves! Look, Prof, when's all this due to happen? When? Bang?' She pointed to the clock and a calendar.

He flew into a complicated explanation; they could understand only about one word in eighteen. They gathered there was some final calculation to be made, and then he kept saying, 'Expectness skepp coming.'

'Oh, I know,' Dido said at last. 'He's waiting for the ship, the *Dark Diamond*. She's bringing the cannonball.'

'So, is so!' He counted on his fingers. 'Tvo, tree day.'

'Three days? We've not got much time, then. Lucky Doc Mayhew's coming back. And then you sail away in the ship, do you?'

'Skepp awaits hjere.' He demonstrated on the map that the *Dark Diamond*, having delivered the cannonball, would hurry round to the other side of Cape Cod to avoid any tidal waves caused by the sudden displacing of Nantucket, and, when things had settled down, would collect the professor and take him home.

'Lucky thing!' said Dido with envy.

'You wishing withcome? I fixing.'

Pen gave Dido an anxious look but did not speak.

'Oh, goodness,' Dido said. 'Thanks, Professor, but I can't leave till Pen's fixed up. Anyway, I'd just as soon not sail along o' Mr Slighcarp.' Or Auntie Trib, she thought. 'Much obliged for the offer though.'

The professor now politely took his leave, indicating that he would return next day to collect his dried clothes. He offered handfuls of golden guineas to the girls, but they shook their heads.

'Not if they're your pay for blowing up poor old kingy,' Dido said; Professor Breadno beamed at her uncomprehendingly, kissed her hand again, murmuring, 'Excellenzchildren,' and trotted off down the hill.

'Well!' Left alone the girls stared at one another in amazement.

'I *said* they was a peevy lot,' Dido remarked at length. 'But I never thought they was as peevy as that. Blowing up St James's Palace!'

'And moving our island! Without so much as a by your leave!'

There came a tap at the door. Both girls jumped guiltily but it was only Nate.

'Anyone in?' he said, putting his head round the door. 'Say, girls! Guess the news! Guess who's turned up!'

'The *Sarah Casket*?'

Dido wondered if it could be the real Aunt Tribulation but did not say so.

'No, it ain't that. It's the old pink 'un!'

'The pink whale?'

'Where is she?'

'Off Squam Head, as plain as plain. She's a-diving and a-playing and a-carrying on like a porpoise; everyone from Polpis has been there watching all afternoon. Doc Mayhew's given strict instructions no one's to hurt her. Is Cap'n Casket awake?'

'I'll see,' said Pen, and ran upstairs.

'He ought to get a sight of her,' Dido said, 'as soon as he is well enough to go out. I dessay she'd do him all the good in the world.'

They tiptoed upstairs after Penitence.

'Papa,' she could be heard saying softly, 'Papa, are you feeling better?'

'Is that thee, Daughter? Why, where am I?'

'In your own bed at home, Papa.'

'Why, so I am. I have been having strange dreams.' He sighed. To Pen's fright, two tears formed in his eyes and rolled slowly down his cheeks. 'I dreamed that I had caught up with her at last,' he said sadly. 'And that she welcomed me.'

'Who, Papa?'

'The pink whale. It was but a dream, though.'

'No, Papa, it wasn't a dream! It was true! And she is waiting for you now, off Squam Head, waiting to see you, so you must hurry and get better,' Pen told him joyfully. But his response was disappointing.

'I know thee does it for the best, Daughter, but thee must not tell falsehoods. There is no pink whale. I have deceived myself for a long time.'

'But, Papa, other people have seen her too. They have said so!'

'They did but mock me.'

'But, Papa, truly she is out there now off Squam Head. Indeed she is!'

Two more tears stood in Captain Casket's eyes but he shook them away angrily, hunched his shoulders, and turned his face to the wall. To all Pen's protestations he would merely reply:

'I do not believe thee.'

Poor Pen came sadly out to the others.

'Never mind,' Dido comforted her. 'Maybe Doc Mayhew'll be able to convince him tomorrow. You make him some nice porridge or broth, summat strengthening, now. Nate'll help me with the chores.'

While they were feeding the animals Dido quickly told Nate about the abominable plan to blow up King James III in his palace, and the disastrous effect this would have on the island of Nantucket.

He whistled in dismay. 'Heave Nantucket right back against the mainland just so's they can swap one king for another? Where's the sense in that? Why don't they stick with the one they've got?'

'Search me,' Dido said. '*I* never heard anything against old James Three. But they've got some George they want to put in.'

'Sounds like plumb foolishness to me,' Nate said.

'Anyway it proves we was right.'

'Did you tell the doc?'

'No,' Dido said crossly. 'He wouldn't listen to me. He thinks little girls tell fairy-tales. You'll have to tell him to-morrow, Nate. Maybe he'll pay attention when he hears Nantucket's going to end up in Atlantic City. I hoped he'd know Aunt Tribulation was a faker, but she turned him off round her finger, smooth as pie, pretending to re-member when he pushed her in the creek. He was fooled.'

'Does Pen know she's really Miss Slighcarp?'

'No,' Dido said. 'I ain't told her. Young Pen's not much on play-acting; she'd give the whole game away.'

'Oh well, I'll be along in the morning early before the doc gets here. 'Night!' Nate jumped on to his pony, which he had left tethered in the yard, and kicked it into a canter.

'Good night,' Dido called. She turned back into the barn to get a basket of eggs for supper – and stood still, petrified with horror. Aunt Tribulation was there, standing in the shadows behind the oil lamp. The upward-slanting light gave her face a most sinister expression.

'Oh!' Dido stammered. 'I d-didn't know – that is, I th-thought you was asleep.'

'I *was* asleep,' Aunt Tribulation said menacingly. 'But I have woken up now, as you see. And I have overheard the most curious conversation!'

As Dido still gazed at her, frozen with indecision – how much had she heard, would there be time to shout after Nate and warn him? – Aunt Tribulation turned her head sharply and said:

'Ebbo, deal with this one. And make no mistake about it – deal with her *for good*!'

A thick black bag came down over Dido's head, smothering her.

9

Kidnapped – Captain Casket is taken for a walk –
Pen meets the doctor – the pink whale meets her friend –
breakfast on the beach

DIDO struggled furiously inside the sack, but somebody had thrust a gag into her mouth (it tasted like and probably was a muddy sock) and her hands were tied in front of her, so she was helpless. When she tried to run somebody tripped her and she fell to the ground and lay there winded and gasping.

Low voices were speaking near by. She heard Aunt Tribulation say:

'Did you get the boy too, brother?'

The answer was a grunt which could have been yes or no.

'That miserable little Breadno has been blabbing,' Aunt Tribulation went on. 'You can never trust scientists or foreigners, curse them! They've no sense. We should have kept a closer watch on him. Luckily it's only got as far as the children; they were to have told Mayhew tomorrow. That has been stopped in time. But Breadno is too big a risk; he'll have to be dealt with too. Has he finished his final calculations?'

'He's just sighting the gun now, and calculating the charge, back at the hut,' Mr Slighcarp's voice said. 'We'll make him work right through the night; it shouldn't take him more than another three or four hours. But sister, are you sure we shall be able to fire the gun without him?'

'Of course we shall, ninnyhammer,' she said impatiently. 'Anybody can let off a gun once it is aimed and the amount of charge is calculated. He'll be no loss. In any case I was planning to leave him behind on the island after the gun was fired; there'd have been little sense in risking our necks coming back to pick him up. I'll fire it, if you like; only mind you pick *me* up.'

'Very well.' He sounded relieved at this suggestion. 'The rest of us will go on board *Dark Diamond* as soon as the gun is loaded, and stand off round Cape Cod in case of tidal waves. Then we'll come back afterwards to pick you up, wherever you've got to. What shall we do with the prisoners, take them on the ship too?'

'Has she been sighted yet?'

'No, I can't think what delays her,' he said vexedly.

'Storms, perhaps. In any case,' said the false Aunt Tribulation, 'there'd be no point in taking the prisoners on board. We don't want to keep them; we want to get rid of them. Tie a rock to their feet and drop them over Sankaty cliff when the tide is high.'

Dido's hair stood on end when she heard this cold-blooded order. She struggled fiercely and bit her gag but in vain.

'Supposing the professor doesn't finish his sums till tomorrow morning? We can hardly toss them over the cliff in broad daylight. There might be people about watching for the whale.'

'Shut them in the lighthouse till dark, then,' she said impatiently. 'The lighthouse keeper goes off at dawn and you know where he keeps the key.'

'Yes, under one of the rocks. That would answer,' he said, considering. 'What about the third child – Casket's daughter –'

Dido held her breath.

'I heard the other girl say she knows nothing.' Dido breathed again, remembering how she had told Nate in the barn that Pen was unaware of Aunt Tribulation's real identity. Evidently Aunt Tribulation had taken this to mean that Pen knew nothing about the plot at all. Lucky for Pen, Dido thought.

'She had better be left here,' Aunt Tribulation went on. 'Doctor Mayhew, when he returns, would think it strange if she were not in attendance on her father.'

'On you, you mean,' Mr Slighcarp said sourly. 'Oh, yes, it's very nice for you up here, waited on hand and foot by those children, while we pig it in the forest!'

'Don't be ridiculous, brother. You know it was quite out of the question that I should camp with you in the forest; it would be most unsuitable.' He made a sneering remark, but she ignored it and said, 'I will think of some story to account for the absence of the other two, should anyone ask.'

'Casket knows nothing about us?'

'Not he. His wits are clean gone.'

'It must have been a shock for you when he turned up.'

'In his present state, it was all for the best,' she said calmly. 'If my own *brother* accepts me, no one else can have any doubts.'

'Suppose he recovers?'

'He is hardly likely to do so before we leave. He keeps jabbering blubber-headed stuff about pink whales.'

'That's not so blubber-headed,' Mr Slighcarp said dryly. 'She's there off Squam Head. There were crowds on the shore yesterday watching her. If she comes farther south we may have to change our plans; we can hardly unload the stuff from *Dark Diamond* with a whole lot of jobberknolls watching.'

'In that case you'd better choose some other point to dispose of the prisoners.'

'It will be all right after nightfall,' he said. 'And we must be at Sankaty, anyway, to watch for the ship; we arranged to exchange signals there; then she'll heave-to a mile off the coast and we'll go out by boat, as if we were after bass, and collect the stuff.'

'Very well. Send me a message as soon as she is sighted. You'd better get back to Breadno now and see that he is kept to work and doesn't wander off again looking for night hawks or something else foolish. The sooner those prisoners are disposed of, the easier I shall feel; we don't want fuss and inquiries at this end spoiling our plans at the last minute.'

Dido was now rudely dragged to her feet, and forced to walk by repeated prods in the back. She could not see because of the sack over her head (it was a flour sack and she kept sneezing as the loose flour sifted down). Her bound hands were buckled on to a dangling strap. In a moment she realized that this was the pony's stirrup. So they must have got Nate, she thought dismally; he's probably on the other side of the pony. Now we are in the basket. How the mischief will we get out of this fix? What'll Pen do when I don't come back? Aunt Tribulation will tell her some tale, so she won't worry for hours. Will she have the sense to tell Doc Mayhew about the gun when he comes tomorrow? Yes, she'll probably have that much sense, but will Doc Mayhew believe her? And suppose Aunt Tribulation catches her at it? And even if he does believe her, that probably won't be in time to help Nate and me and poor old Breadno. We'll be feeding the fishes before they guess what's happened unless we can work ourselves loose somehow. Oh well; let's hope old Breadno takes a devil of a long time over those final calculations of his.

Immersed in these gloomy thoughts she trudged along. The going was much rougher now; they had left the track. Bushes and brambles caught her legs, so she guessed they must be approaching the forest. Presently they halted and there was a long wait while the pony stamped and shifted impatiently. Dido was desperately tired and longed to sit down, but the strap that attached her hands to the stirrup was too short to allow this; all she could do was to lean against the pony, grateful for its warmth in the chilly night air. In the end she did fall into a sort of doze on her feet, regardless of the awkward position. When she next opened her eyes she was surprised to find daylight filtering through the loose mesh of the flour sack. Presently footsteps approached and there were some faint protesting cries which ceased abruptly; evidently poor Professor Breadno had been added to the roll of prisoners. Dido felt sorry for him and remorseful that she had been the cause of the gang's decision to dispose of him. But, she thought, he shouldn't have invented the gun. I suppose he don't see the harm in it; he's like a child.

Now the procession moved forward steadily for a considerable distance; Dido, stiff and aching all over, thought they might have gone three or four miles when at length they halted again and their captors conferred in low voices.

'Too late to chuck 'em now; broad daylight and somebody might come along. Besides, it ain't full tide yet; no water at the foot of the cliff.'

Thank the lord Breadno's a slow worker, Dido thought.

'Any sign of the ship yet?'

'Yes, there's a sail to south'ards that looks like her.'

'What the blazes is she doing down thataway? No wonder she's behind schedule.'

'Gale blew her off course, maybe.'

'Has the lighthouse keeper left yet?'

'Yes, half an hour ago.'

'Bring them along, then; best carry them the last bit. Lucky we put them in flour bags and the weather's a bit thick; if anyone happens along, we're just delivering flour to the lighthouse.'

Mr Slighcarp laughed sourly.

Dido was picked up and slung over somebody's shoulder, carried about a hundred yards in a very jolting and uncomfortable manner, and then thumped down roughly on to a stone floor. Something – another body – fell heavily on top of her. She wondered if it was Nate or Breadno. Then she heard footsteps retreating. A door slammed. I'll count to a hundred, she decided; then I'll try to wriggle out of my sack. Dunno when I've been so tired, though.

Counting was a mistake. The numbers slipped by more and more slowly...tied themselves in knots...began to run backwards. Before she had reached forty, Dido was asleep.

The pony's footsteps had died away down the track. Aunt Tribulation turned and went back into the house. A delicious smell of broth filled the kitchen. She could hear the voice of Penitence upstairs in Captain Casket's room.

'Try to take a little more, Papa dear! To please me! Just a spoonful and a cracker. That's it – famous! Now you may lie down and sleep.'

In a moment or two Pen appeared, looking very white and fatigued, with the empty bowl and plate.

'Well, miss!' Aunt Tribulation snapped. 'I notice you make broth for your father but none for your poor old aunt who's had charge of you all this time. Fine gratitude, I must say!'

'I'm sorry, Aunt,' Penitence said tiredly. She pushed the hair off her forehead. 'There is plenty more broth in the pot if you would like it. I can heat it up in a moment.'

'Very well. Make haste!'

'Yes, Aunt.' And Pen added gently, looking Aunt Tribulation straight in the face, 'Poor Aunt, is your rheumatism very bad?'

'Mind your own business, miss!'

'Where's Dido?' Pen asked, as she put the broth pot on the stove.

'The sow got loose again. Nate offered to help her search and they may not be back for a long time. You had best go to bed when you have washed up those dishes.'

'I shall sit with Papa.' Penitence poured broth into a bowl, adding a pinch of herbs and spices, and set it before Aunt Tribulation.

Then she quietly said good night and went up to the captain's room.

Aunt Tribulation sat at the kitchen table, grim and erect; slowly, because it was so hot, she sipped at the steaming broth.

Captain Casket suddenly woke up and looked about his room. The whale-oil lamp was still burning brightly, but daylight was beginning to creep past the curtains. He saw his daughter Penitence sitting at the foot of the bed. She was very pale.

'How do you feel now, Papa?' she asked in a low voice.

'I am better, Daughter, I thank thee, after that excellent broth and the good sleep it brought. I feel myself again.'

'Do you *indeed*, Papa? Truly? Well enough to get up and take a walk?'

'Take a walk?' he repeated in bewilderment. 'Why, what o'clock is it, then?'

'Not long after dawn.'

'Strange time for a walk, Daughter.'

'No, Papa, it is very urgent – it is dreadfully important. Can you, do you think? Can you try?'

'What for, my child?'

'I will tell you when we are on our way. Please, Papa! I would not ask you if it were not so important. But if you cannot come I shall have to go on my own, and I do not like to leave you.'

Captain Casket sat up and found himself fairly strong. 'I shall do well enough, I thank thee, child,' he said, when Pen offered to help him dress, so she retreated to the kitchen and packed a bag of food.

'Why, who is this?' Captain Casket said when he came downstairs.

'Hush!'

Penitence laid her finger on her lips and dragged him to the door. 'I will tell you outside.' He followed her, puzzled but complying.

When they were well away from the farm Pen turned to

the right and took the track leading towards Sankaty.

'Now!' she said. 'I will explain everything, Papa. But first, did you really not know that lady sleeping in the kitchen?'

'Never saw her in my life before,' declared Captain Casket.

'She is not my Aunt Tribulation?'

'That lady? No indeed, nor in the least like her! Tribulation is much shorter, with black hair and eyes.'

'Is she? I had not remembered. Well, Papa, that lady has been calling herself Aunt Tribulation and living at the farm for the last month.'

'I do not understand!' he said, passing a hand over his forehead. 'Passing herself off as my sister Tribulation? But that is infamous behaviour! Then where is my sister?'

'I do not know, Papa.'

'This is an outrage! We must go back at once and demand to know what she means by it, and where Tribulation is. Some harm may have come to her.'

'Wait, Papa, listen. I have not told you all yet. That is not nearly the worst. Yesterday Dido and I helped a man who had fallen into the cranberry bog. He is Professor Breadno, a foreign scientist, and he has made a gun in the Hidden Forest which is going to shoot a shot right across to London and kill the king of England.'

Captain Casket sat down abruptly in a clump of broom.

'I am *not* better,' he said mournfully. 'I am having wild delusions. I think my own daughter is telling me about a gun which will fire across the Atlantic. Next I shall be seeing pink whales.'

Pen pulled him to his feet.

'Yes, you will, Papa, but please listen, this is true! It is a wicked plot by the English Hanoverians to get rid of King James.'

'But why,' asked her father doggedly, 'not that I believe a word of this, mind thee, but why do they come all the way to Nantucket to fire at King James? Why not just do it across the Thames?'

'Why,' Pen said impatiently, 'because nobody over here will bother to stop them. Whereas in London I suppose the king's soldiers would grab them if they so much as showed their faces. But that is not the worst, Papa.'

'Speak on then, Daughter.'

'Last night,' said Pen breathlessly, 'I went out to the barn for some eggs and what do you think I saw? The woman who calls herself Aunt Tribulation was there, and she and Mr Slighcarp put a sack over poor Dido's head and tied her hands up with rope, and I heard Aunt Tribulation say that Dido and Nate were to be thrown over Sankaty cliff.'

'Why should they want to do that?' asked Captain Casket in perplexity.

'Because Dido and Nate had found out about their gun and were going to get Doctor Mayhew to stop them. And that woman who pretends to be Aunt Tribulation is really Mr Slighcarp's sister. I heard her call him brother.'

'Slighcarp? Is he, too, involved in this? I always thought him a sly, foxy-faced fellow. I was glad enough when he failed to turn up for this trip.'

'Mr Slighcarp was helping get the gun ready in the Hidden Forest. Oh, Papa, I was so frightened when I heard the things they said! I nearly screamed out to them to let poor Dido and Nate go, but I knew they would only put *my* head in a bag too, and then there would be nobody to help them, or to look after you, Papa.'

'So what did thee do then, Daughter?'

'I crept away in the shadows – it is fortunate that I am not very big. And, then, luckily, Aunt Tribulation – I mean Miss Slighcarp – asked me for some of your broth. So I gave her some of the poppy juice that Doctor Mayhew had left for you in it, and she went off to sleep in the kitchen as you saw.' Here Penitence could not help giggling at the thought of having successfully put Aunt Tribulation to sleep.

'Dear me, Daughter. Was that judicious?'

'But, Papa, what else could I do? They are going to throw Dido and Nate and Professor Breadno off Sankaty cliffs unless we do something to stop them. So as soon as Aunt Trib – Mr Slighcarp's sister – was asleep and you were peaceful, Papa, I crept out of the house and went to the forest and warned the professor to take as long over his calculations as he possibly could. I do not think he precisely understood why I wished him to do so, but when I explained that the lives of my friends depended on it, and gave him some molasses candy, he agreed.'

'Thee went to the camp of these villains in the forest? But, Daughter, was thee not afraid?'

'Yes I was,' Penitence said in a low tone. 'I was dreadfully afraid.'

'And did the others not stop thee speaking to this man?'

'No, because they had left him alone in a little hut and were sitting outside round a fire. So I stole in very quietly and he was very surprised to see me.'

'Alack!' said Captain Casket. He had halted, leaning heavily on his daughter's shoulder. 'Child, I am not so well as I thought. I must sit and rest awhile. Perhaps thee had best go on to Sankaty without me. Yet what can one frail child do against such evil? I shall be in dread for thee.' His legs failed him and he sank into a clump of bayberry.

'Oh, Papa!' cried Penitence in distress. 'Can you really go no farther? Look, it is not much more than a mile now to Sankaty, you can see the white tower.'

'Child, I have outplayed my strength. The fever was a short one but sharp while it lasted.'

'Oh, what shall I do?' Penitence wrung her hands. 'I shall have to go on, Papa. I must try to help Dido and Nate. They have been so good to me.'

'Yes, thee must. I shall pray for thy safe return. Ask help

of anyone thee may encounter – yet it is not likely that many will be abroad at this hour,' he said doubtfully.

'There may be some,' said Pen with more optimism. 'Because of the pi – ' She checked herself, gave her father a tender kiss, and hurried on towards the foot of the slope at the top of which Sankaty lighthouse stood on the cliff edge like a pointing finger.

By great good luck Penitence had not gone far when she heard the thud of hoofs. Crossing her path ahead lay the road from Polpis to Sankaty; to her left she saw a cart proceeding at a smart pace. By running her fastest and waving a handkerchief she was able to attract the attention of the driver who slowed to a halt as she reached the road.

'Well, bless my soul if it isn't little Penitence Casket!' cried a cheerful voice. 'What are you doing out so early? Like all the rest of Nantucket, come for a sight of the pink whale? She's a bit farther up the coast, child, towards Squam, but heading this way. How's my patient this morning?'

It was Doctor Mayhew, driving Mungo.

'Oh, Doctor Mayhew!' cried Pen thankfully. 'I was never so glad to see anybody in all my life, never! Will you help me, please?'

'Of course I will, child. I was just on my way to visit your father, soon as I've seen a patient in 'Sconset. I spent the night at Polpis and then, thought I, I'll just have another look at this famous pink whale and, if she's still there and old Jabez Casket is able, I'll take him to see her; a sight like that might be just the thing to put him on his legs again.'

'Oh yes!' cried Pen. 'It was what I thought, too! But when I told Papa that she had been seen he would not believe me.'

'He'll believe the evidence of his own eyes, I suppose. And ears. Listen!'

They both stood silent. Above the hushing of the sea

beyond the cliff could be heard a strange noise – a most mournful bellow, rising sometimes to a whistle, then sinking again to a kind of discontented mutter.

'What is it?'

'Why, it's the old pink 'un, grizzling away out there in the ocean. It's my belief,' continued the doctor, 'that she misses your pa and is a-calling for him. And the sooner he sees her the better, in my opinion.'

'Will you help me fetch him?' Pen said eagerly. 'He is not far from here. We started to walk to Sankaty but Papa's strength failed him.'

'Walk to Sankaty? Child, are you out of your wits? What possessed you to do such a thing?'

'Oh, sir, there are wicked men on Nantucket who are going to throw Dido and Nate into the sea off Sankaty cliff. They have shut them up in the lighthouse till this evening. Will you help me let them out?'

'Eh, bless my soul,' the doctor said in astonishment. 'What imaginations you young 'uns do have. Only yesterday that friend of yours was telling me all about some gun in the forest. Says I, that's no gun, child, but the biggest telescope between here and California.'

'But it *is* a gun! They *are* in the lighthouse! If you come with me you will see!'

'Dear, dear,' said the doctor. 'Ah well, I always say it does no harm to humour people in their fancies. What shall we do first, then, pick your father up or go to the lighthouse?'

'Oh, the lighthouse, please!' Pen said, clutching his arm in her anxiety. 'Every moment may be important.'

'Very well, we'll see how fast this canny old mule of yours can go if he's pushed.'

Mungo was cooperative and it took them only another five minutes to gallop up the hill to the lighthouse. The place seemed totally deserted. A chill wind blew the grasses and straggling shrubs which covered the sandhills round about; beyond the low cliff the ocean growled and whispered. The desolate bellow of the pink whale could still be heard farther north.

'Oh, quick!' whispered Pen, as the doctor tied Mungo to a railing. 'Suppose we are too late!'

'What about the key, child?'

'I heard Mr Slighcarp say that it was kept under a rock.'

'It'll be close by the door, I reckon,' grunted the doctor, and soon found it. 'Well, now, where's these poor castaway captives of yours?' He thrust the big key into the lock, turned it, and pushed open the heavy door. 'Anybody about?' he called, and walked in, with Pen close at his heels.

The round room was empty.

'You see,' Dr Mayhew said indulgently. 'All imagination, as I was say – '

Pen had darted in horror to a pile of flour-sacks and bits of rope. '*Look!*' White as a sheet she held up a length of rope. 'There's blood on this! Doctor Mayhew! Do you think they've thrown them over already?'

'Thrown – hey! Let's have a look at that rope. Yes, that's blood sure enough,' he muttered, inspecting it. 'And recent, too, it's hardly dry. What in tarnation's name has been going on around here? Can there be some truth in the child's story?' He stared at her in doubt.

'Hush!' whispered Pen with terrified eyes. 'What's that sound?'

They listened and both heard it: a step on the winding stair overhead.

Then all of a sudden a voice burst into song:

'As I was a-walking down Wauwinet way
I met a young maiden and this she did say:
Oh, Pocomo's pretty and Quidnet is quaint
But the swimming on Surfside is fit for a saint!

'And Madaket's modish and 'Sconset's sedate
And Shimmo is sheltered and Great Point is great – '

'*Nate!*' cried Pen. 'Nate, is that you?'

'It's never Penitence?' He came clattering down the stair and into sight. 'And Doc Mayhew too! Well, of all the luck! Chop me into chowder, how ever did you get here?'

'Where's the others? Where's Dido? And Professor Breadno?'

'Just a-coming down,' he said grinning. 'It's a powerful long stair. We'd been up top, trying to work out whether, if we tied all the bits of rope together, they'd be long enough to let one of us down to unlock the door from the outside. Dido thought yes. Professor Breadno thought not. I'm glad we didn't have to try. Hey!' he yelled up the stair. 'Pen's here with the doc. Come on down!'

'*Penny!*'

Dido shot down the last round of the spiral stair like a whirlwind, threw herself at Pen, and hugged her. 'How did you do it? How did you know we was here? You *clever* little girl, Pen!'

Doctor Mayhew was staring at Nate's wrists. 'So that's where the blood came from! Hey, boy, who's been gnawing at you?'

'Well, you see, sir, we was tied up. Dido and I managed to shuffle the sacks off each other's heads – that took a plaguy long time, I can tell you – but we couldn't get our ropes undone, not nohow. So I rubbed through mine on the edge of the bottom stair, but it left my wrists kind of chawed-up.'

'And then he undid me and the professor,' Dido explained.

'I'll put something on those wrists for you right away, my boy. But where are the miscreants now?'

'They sighted their schooner, the *Dark Diamond*. I heard them talking outside. They were planning to go out to her in a dory, as if they was after fish. Guess that's the dory you can see about a mile to south'ards now. We kept out of view in case it was them. You can get a famous view of the old pink 'un from the top of the tower; she's running down this way like a Saratoga winner – hear her bellow?'

'Ja – hwalnn!' exclaimed Professor Breadno enthusiastically. 'Ismistibiggn hwalln!' He had been more than a little subdued since his recent experience, but the sight of Rosie appeared to have cheered him up.

'Oh, this is Professor Breadno,' Nate told the doctor. 'He was going to let off the gun for the Hanoverians, but he told Dido and Pen about it, so his friends fixed to chuck him over the cliff in case he told anyone else. Nice lot, ain't they?'

'So there really is a gun, my boy? It is not a telescope, not a fairy-tale of the young ladies?'

'Oh no, it's there right enough, sir. And the Professor says it's capable of firing across to London.'

'Königsbang, monstershoot,' the professor put in proudly.

'So we've got to stop them, haven't we?' Dido said.

'Well, but that ain't so easy, my dear,' Doctor Mayhew objected. 'For one thing, it's none of our affair if the English choose to blow each other up. For another, there's precious few able-bodied men on the island – every man-jack of them is off whaling and we've nothing but young children and old crocks like myself, and whale-widows.'

'But Doctor!' exclaimed Pen. 'You haven't heard the worst yet! When those wicked men let off the gun it will blow Nantucket right back against the mainland – right back to Atlantic City!'

Doctor Mayhew slowly turned purple. It was a fearsome sight.

'*What did you say?*' he bellowed. 'Just repeat that, will you?'

'It's true, Doc!'

There were maps and charts on the wall. Professor Breadno was pleased to demonstrate how, when the shot was fired across Nova Scotia, the back-thrust would send the island of Nantucket sliding south-westwards to bump against the New Jersey coast.

'She ain't so tight on her moorings, I guess,' Nate said. 'Being mostly sand.'

'Great guns! Why didn't you tell me that before? *Push our island over against that crowd of money-grabbing roustabouts and frauds at Atlantic City?* Why, we'd have a lawsuit from here to doomsday before we ever got it out of their clutches again. What would all the whaling captains say to me when they came back from their voyages and found Nantucket had moved? This puts a different complexion on the whole matter!'

'What'll we do, then?'

'We'll have to go into it very thoroughly,' Doctor Mayhew said, taking deep breaths to calm himself down.

Here Penitence said in a small voice, 'Please, what about Papa?'

The doctor started.

'Quite right, my dear, quite right. In the emotion of the moment I had forgotten about him. We must go to his aid at once. Nate, just run and make sure those scoundrels are well away so that we can leave the lighthouse in safety.'

Nate soon reported that both the *Dark Diamond* and the dory had shifted south; the *Dark Diamond* was almost out of sight round the corner of the island at Tom Never's Head, and the dory was pursuing her.

'Guess they don't want to get mixed up with the old pink 'un,' he said. 'She's middling close now; hear her whistle?'

Indeed the whale was now letting off regular blasts, like the siren of a lightship, almost as if she were trying to attract somebody's attention. With one accord the whole party moved outside to look at her.

'Why, there's Papa!' cried Pen joyfully. 'He must have felt himself sufficiently rested to follow me. Papa, Papa! Do you feel all right now? Are you sure that you have not overtired yourself?'

'No, Daughter, no,' Captain Casket said absently. He moved towards the group.

The hillside where they stood sloped up quite steeply past the lighthouse to the cliff-edge, so that it was not possible to get a view of the sea until one stood on the very summit.

'What is that sound?' said Captain Casket.

'Take care, Papa!' cried Pen anxiously. She darted to him and held his arm, supporting him tenderly. They moved on together and stood at the top of the cliff.

A great sigh burst from Captain Casket.

'Oh!' he said brokenly. 'I am dreaming again. I must be! But it is a beautiful dream!'

'No, Papa, it is no dream! We all see her too.'

'And ain't she half carrying on,' said Dido. 'Gosh-swoggle, ain't she got no *dignity*? You'd think a grown whale would be ashamed to act so.'

The pink whale was indeed giving an exuberant display of rapture at meeting her old friend Captain Casket. It was a beautiful and touching sight. She leapt clean out of the water a great many times, as if bent on demonstrating how high she could go; she repeatedly dived and came up, she rolled playfully from side to side waving her flukes and, as Dido said, 'ogling the captain like an orange-girl'.

'I must go down to her,' Captain Casket said.

'Pray be very careful, Papa!'

'Why don't we all go down?' Doctor Mayhew suggested. 'Didn't I see you with a basket of food, Pen? How about breakfast on the beach? Those ruffians are not likely to come back while *she's* out there. And it's not a sight to miss.'

So Pen fetched the food from the cart while Dido and Nate prospected for a path down the cliff, and then the

whole party descended to the beach. Captain Casket made straight for the edge of the ocean, and Pen had much ado to prevent his wading in, so eager was he to approach as close as possible to the pink whale – who, luckily, saw his intention and swam in near to the land; and so these two friends gazed at one another with the utmost delight and mutual satisfaction.

'Could you give her a hint not to come too close, sir?' Nate said anxiously. 'It'd be the devil to pay dragging her off if she got beached; I dare say she'll weigh all of a hundred and fifty tons.'

'She is a fine figure of a whale,' murmured Captain Casket blissfully. But he roused himself to make some warning gestures, and the pink whale evidently understood these, for she swam to and fro parallel with the shore, letting out a series of loving bellows, without coming too near.

'Well, it's most uncommon I'm bound to say,' Dido remarked. 'But if I don't get summat to eat soon you might jist as well bury me on this beach, for I shan't be able to climb up the cliff again. What've you got in your basket, Penny?'

Pen had large numbers of hard-boiled eggs and buttered biscuits, molasses tarts, and a stone jug of broth for the Captain which Dido and Nate heated up over a driftwood fire. The broth was all he would take; after that he stood at the edge of the surf throwing hard-boiled eggs to Rosie, who caught them with the grace of a dolphin. Doctor Mayhew opened his black bag and brought out a large leather bottle of ginger-jub which he passed round for the party's refreshment.

'Never go on my rounds without it,' he said. 'If medicine won't help a man, this will. Many's the fellow digging clams today who'd ha' been buried long ago, but for a dram of ginger-jub.' It was indeed powerful stuff.

While they were eating, Dido said:

'Now, Penny, I wants to hear all about how you came to be trapesing over the moors at sun-up with your pa, a-rarin' to rescue us, instead of snoring in your bed like a good girl. How the mischief did you know where we was?'

Pen explained how she had overheard the scene in the barn.

'And you mean to say you bamboozled old Misery so she never guessed you knew? Why, Pen, I never thought you had it in you,' exclaimed Dido handsomely. 'You're a walking wonder, girl! And slipped a Mickey Finn in her skilly? She'll surely think she's got sleeping sickness! Oh, dear, I haven't laughed so much since Mr Slighcarp fell over the cutting-spade!'

'Order!' said Doctor Mayhew severely. 'Now, has

everybody finished eating? Nate! Stop throwing eggs at the whale. This is a serious occasion. We have got to think how to prevent those deadbeats from heaving our island into the middle of New Jersey!'

10

Ways and means – Penitence eavesdrops –
Aunt Tribulation is suspicious – the rocket –
the gun's last ride

'Now,' said Doctor Mayhew, absently tipping the last of
the ginger-jub down his gullet, 'how are we going to stop
them firing this gun?'

'Is not firing kungscannon?' exclaimed Professor
Breadno woefully. 'Is not having bigbang?'

'Your big bang, my dear professor, would leave this
island in a devilish undesirable location.'

'Could firing otherwards round world mayhaps?' the
Professor said hopefully. 'I fixing nordwestbang.'

'No, no, professor, that would push us out into the
middle of the Atlantic, right over to Spain probably. Can't
you see, we don't want the gun fired at *all*.'

The professor's face fell.

'Besides,' Dido pointed out kindly, 'you really can't
shoot poor old King James, you know!'

'Na, na, na, snat Kung Jimsbangen, 'sKung George-
bangen. Kung George IV!'

'King George the Fourth?' said Dido, bewildered. 'But
we haven't *got* a King George! It's King James the Third,
bless his wig!'

The professor shook his head and burst into a flood of
refutal, mostly in his own incomprehensible language,
which it took some time to disentangle.

'I see what it is,' Dido said at length. 'Those peevy culls
have been leading him up the garden path, making him
believe there was a Hanoverian king on the throne because
he's really *against* the Hanoverians and they wanted him to

make the gun for them. Talking about pitching the double! What a lot of swindlers! Can you explain to him, Doc?'

It took some time to get across to the professor that there was already the sort of king he preferred on the English throne and therefore no need to shoot anyone off it; in the end he was convinced but greatly disappointed.

'Firing at sönn, at mönn, at stare?' he suggested as a last forlorn hope.

'No, Breadno, that just *wouldn't do*. It would sink us. We'd go right under water. Have a bit of sense, can't you?'

Poor Professor Breadno sighed heavily and stumped away from the council down to the edge of the waves, where he stood skipping stones and gazing mournfully at Rosie, who, exhausted by her great aquabatic display, was resting comfortably in the swell, her tiny eyes fixed on Captain Casket with a look of great devotion.

'You say the gun is now all ready to fire, and the professor's presence is not needed?' Doctor Mayhew said to Dido.

'That's right. Aunt Trib – Miss Slighcarp said she would fire it. They only need the cannonball and that's being delivered today. Then they plan to go back on board the ship, tipping us over the cliff on the way, I dessay, and skedaddle till the rumpus has died down, before coming back to pick up the gunner. They wasn't aiming to pick poor old Breadno up at all; I wonder if they'll leave Auntie Trib behind too?'

'So,' said Doctor Mayhew thoughtfully, 'as we haven't enough able-bodied men on the island to deal with a whole shipload of desperate ruffians, our best plan would be somehow to get rid of the gun itself before they can fire it.'

'But, Doc, it's *huge*! It's about a mile long, and as thick as a tree! I don't see how you'll ever get it moved if you've got no help but grannies and young 'uns and whaling widders.'

'No more do I at present,' Doctor Mayhew said frankly.

'But somehow it must be done, so we had all better set our wits to work.'

For a long time nobody spoke. They sat frowning in the silence of intense thought.

'We couldn't stuff the barrel full o' summat?' Dido suggested doubtfully.

'That might lead to a most disastrous explosion,' Doctor Mayhew said.

'Cut the gun into sections – no, that would take too long,' Nate muttered.

Several hours slipped by in fruitless discussion. Nate paced about the beach in circles, staring at the ground.

At last Pen said, 'Sheep.'

'Sheep, Penny?'

'There are such a lot on the island. Could they not be put to some use? Harnessed to the gun and made to drag it away?'

'Dunnamany ropes you'd need,' Dido said kindly. 'Have another try.'

Nate, who had wandered near, strolled down to the edge of the waves and skipped stones with the professor.

'Or we could bury – no, that would not do,' Pen sighed in discouragement.

'Hallo, what's bitten Nate and the professor?' Dido suddenly said.

Nate, apparently galvanized by an idea, had grabbed the professor's arm and was talking to him earnestly, using a lot of gestures, sometimes pointing out to sea. They buttonholed Captain Casket, and brought him into the discussion. He nodded, at first doubtfully, then with confidence and animation.

'What's the lay?' called Dido. Nate came pounding back over the shingle with the others close behind him.

'We've got it! The very thing! We'll use the pink 'un.'

'Old Rosie?' said Dido. 'Why, o' course! She's just the

article. Why in Pharaoh's name didn't I think of that meself?'

'But how? How do you mean?' said Pen.

'Why, it was your notion of the sheep that put it into my head,' Nate told her. 'Tie a rope to her flukes, don't you see, and get her to haul the gun into the sea. It'd be as easy as a greased slide.'

'But would it be *kind*?' said Penitence dubiously.

'We can fix a knot that'll come undone as soon as the gun's in the sea. Cap'n Casket's agreeable to the idea. Says he don't think it'd upset her too much.'

'We'd need an uncommonly strong rope, and a long one,' Doctor Mayhew observed.

'There's the lifeguard rope,' Nate said. 'That's best new five-inch Manila, and there's nigh on two mile of it.'

'We'll need all of that. Now let's think of how we'd go about this. One party would have to make an end of the rope fast to the gun, while Captain Casket and somebody else must row out to the whale with the other end. We can use the lifeguard's dory – I'll explain to him afterwards. I had best be with the captain, who must obviously remain here on the shore so that the whale does not swim away before we are ready. Nate, you had better go with Professor Breadno and tie the rope to the gun; the professor will know the most suitable place to make fast.'

Nate saw a difficulty.

'How're we going to shift the rope? That coil's powerful heavy.'

'In Mungo's cart,' Dido suggested. 'We can all lift it in, and then it will unroll as you go.'

'We can't take the cart all the way to the forest; if there's anybody left on guard they'd spot us.'

'No, but you'll have unrolled a lot of rope by the time you get there, it won't be so heavy. You can leave the cart about half a mile away and roll the coil along the last bit. There are sheepskins in the cart; put those on your shoulders and meander through the scrub a bit aimless-like and stooping; anybody watching from the forest'll think you're a sheep. I'll come with you to keep a lookout,' Dido volunteered.

'We really ought to try to find out when they aim to fire,' Doctor Mayhew said. 'If Miss Slighcarp's going to do it, we only have to keep an eye on her movements, and as soon as she starts for the forest we'll know. Who could do that?'

All eyes turned on poor Penitence, who became rather pale, swallowed once or twice, and then said valiantly, 'I'll do it. I don't mind. That is if, Doctor Mayhew, you'll promise to look after Papa.'

'Penny you're a real bang-up hero,' Dido said warmly. 'I wish I could come with you, but if Aunt Trib was to see I'd got out of the lighthouse she'd twig the whole lay in a minute. But you can pretend you know nothing about anything and just act like a saphead – try to delay her from going to the forest if she seems liable to start before Nate and the cap'n are ready and we've got the gun away.'

'How should I delay her?' asked Pen nervously.

'Why, talk to her, distract her, ask her advice about summat – ask her how to make wedding cake or some blame thing.'

'And supposing she wants to know where I've been and where Papa is, what shall I tell her?'

'Why, you can tell the truth. Say Doc Mayhew reckoned as how it would do your pa good to have a look at the pink whale and that he's a-sitting on Sankaty beach. That sounds innocent and harmless and will put her off the scent.'

'Very well,' said Pen, wan but resolute.

Everything was now in train. The whole party helped to lift the lifeguard rope, which was kept coiled in a chest at the foot of the lighthouse, on to Mungo's cart. Then Doctor Mayhew and Captain Casket returned to the beach, dragging with them one end of the rope, while Nate, Dido, and Professor Breadno drove slowly away down the Polpis road, unrolling the coil as they went. They took Pen with them for some way, and then she left them and struck off across the moors towards Soul's Hill.

'Poor Penny,' said Dido who waved vigorously as Pen looked back for reassurance. 'I reckoned as how I'd teach her to stand up to Aunt Tribulation, but I never figured things would be quite as rugged as this. But she's coming up smiling, I will say; I'd never a thought Pen had so much gumption in her. Reckon her pa ought to be mighty well satisfied with her now, considering what a little puny moping thing she was on board ship. If he could take his mind off that blame whale o' hisn for five minutes, that is!'

The whale was still just visible, rocking like a pink blancmange in the breakers, and Nate began singing softly:

'Sweet whale of Nantucket, so rosy and nice,
As round and as pink as a strawberry ice – '

'That ain't stately enough,' Dido said. 'That don't give a proper notion of her at all.'

'All right.' Nate considered a moment or two, while a few more fathoms of rope unrolled.

'How about this, then?

'Sweet Whale of Nantucket, so pink and so round,
The pride of our island, the pearl of the Sound,
By Providence blest to our shores you were led,
Long, long may you gambol off Sankaty Head!'

'That's better,' said Dido. 'Though it was really Cap'n Casket she was led by, not Providence. I guess really, all the time he thought he was following her, *she* was following *him*.'

As Pen disappeared over a hill Dido said with a sudden pang of anxiety, 'Croopus, I do hope nothing don't go wrong when Penny gets to the farm. I wonder did we do right to send her?'

'Oh, I guess she'll be all right,' Nate said.

Dusk had begun to fall when Penitence reached the farm. Nobody was in sight. Penitence slipped quietly into the kitchen and then paused, as she heard voices coming from the parlour. The door was not quite closed.

'. . . should be loaded by now,' Mr Slighcarp's voice said. 'Thanks to that cursed whale and all the brats and old grannies swarming on the beach at Quidnet we were obliged to slip right round to the south side of the island, which meant the men had to carry the shot a great deal farther from the landing-place. We didn't want to risk anyone getting a sight of it.'

'No, you were very right,' his sister agreed. 'Where is *Dark Diamond* now?'

'Making north again, back to Quidnet. Just coasting along she's innocent enough – might be going back for another sight of the pink whale. We've another boat beached at Quidnet ready to take us all off to her when the gun's loaded.'

'What delayed the ship so long?'

'They were chased all the way from Spithead by a perditioned naval sloop, the *Thrush*, which several times nearly caught them; in order to give it the slip they were forced to beat right down to Trinidad.'

'What happened to the sloop, then?' asked Miss Slighcarp uneasily.

'They lost her in the end; probably gave up and went back to report failure.'

'It's as well we are now ready to fire.'

'They could never have touched us on Nantucket; it's American soil. But we had best get away prudently and as fast as possible in case the sloop is still hanging about.'

'What time shall I fire the gun?'

Penitence drew nearer to the door and listened intently.

Mr Slighcarp did some calculating. 'Hmm, there's a fair south-westerly, say fifteen knots, plus the trip to Quidnet

. . . Give us time to get away. Say six hours. Better make it eight hours. Don't fire before midnight.'

'Very well. I will fire at midnight exactly. Darkness suits us better,' she said. 'There is no risk of being seen on my way there. I don't want to be suspected before you come back to pick me up. As Tribulation Casket I am safe enough.'

'Come to think,' he said, 'where is old Casket and the child?'

'Lord knows. The wretched, foggy sea air in this place makes me sleep like the dead; when I woke this morning it was late and they'd gone off somewhere. To see the whale, I suppose. You'll deal with the prisoners?'

'We couldn't just leave them, I suppose?' he said.

'Fool! Use your wits! As soon as they speak to anybody, our whole plan comes crashing down. If the lighthouse keeper sees them – no, they must be dealt with.'

'I'll see to it, then. On the way to the boat. I must hurry. One last thing – '

'Yes?'

The voices were approaching the door and Pen looked desperately round for a hiding-place. There was just time to scramble into the grandfather clock.

'Should any emergency arise, so that it becomes necessary to fire *before* the time agreed, we will communicate by rocket. If we let off a rocket, do you fire as soon as possible afterwards. Likewise, if for some reason you need to fire earlier, send off your rocket first to warn us and we'll make for what shelter we can, wherever we are. But fire at all costs; we shall never have a better chance. The usurping Stuart monarch is bound to be in his palace tonight because tomorrow is the State opening of Parliament.'

'I shall not fail.'

She laid the rocket on the kitchen table and the two of them went out of the house, still talking.

Pen acted on a lightning impulse. She sprang out of the

clock, seized the rocket, which was about the size of a french loaf, and dipped it, first one end, then the other, in a large jug of buttermilk. A bundle of lucifer matches lay with the rocket. She served them in the same manner. There was just time to climb back into the clock before Aunt Tribulation reappeared.

Pen was now in terror lest Aunt Tribulation observe the damp state of the rocket or should take it into her head to wind the clock. Fortunately she did neither of these things, but went upstairs. Seizing the chance Pen slipped out of the house, first cautiously reconnoitring to make sure that Mr Slighcarp had gone. He was visible in the distance, walking down the track to Sankaty at a great pace. Pen re-entered the house, making as much noise as possible, took a deep breath, and called up the stairs:

'Aunt? Aunt Tribulation? Are you there?'

'Penitence? Is that you?'

Aunt Tribulation – somehow Pen could not think of her as Miss Slighcarp – came downstairs, looking grim. To Pen's alarm she had exchanged her usual gingham for a black silk dress and a black, fringed shawl. She carried an awe-inspiring bonnet ornamented with small jet tombstones. She wore bottle-green boots.

'Well!' she said. 'What have you to say for yourself, miss? Where have you been all day? And where is your father?'

'With Doctor Mayhew, ma'am, watching the pink whale. You were asleep when we left – we did not like to disturb you. Doctor Mayhew is keeping Papa on the shore a little longer but they – they thought I should come home. Is Dido not back yet?'

'You can see she is not,' Aunt Tribulation remarked severely. 'Well, child, don't stand gaping – there are plenty of tasks to be done. What's the matter?'

'You are so fine, Aunt!'

'I shall be going out by and by,' Aunt Tribulation said

carelessly. 'Hurry now – feed the animals and make some supper.'

'Yes, ma'am.'

As Pen fed the pigs and hens she was filled with anxious calculations. If Aunt Tribulation did not go off to fire the gun till midnight, that was excellent, for it should give Nate and the Professor ample time to secure the rope, and for the pink whale to do her part. But what would happen when Mr Slighcarp returned to Sankaty lighthouse and found the captives had escaped? Almost certainly he would let off his rocket and Aunt Tribulation, alerted, would start out to fire the gun much earlier. Could she somehow be prevented from hearing or seeing the rocket? Pen hurried back to the house, leaving half the pigs screaming with rage because they had not been fed.

Aunt Tribulation was seated in the kitchen rocker, grimly swaying back and forth while she stared straight ahead; from the expression on her face she might have been enjoying the spectacle of St James's Palace blowing sky-high. Pen began clanking pots and pans, putting bacon to hiss and splutter in a skillet, pounding sugar to break up the lumps.

'Don't make such a noise, child,' Aunt Tribulation said. 'I can't hear myself think. No, don't draw the curtains yet, it is too stuffy, and not quite dark, leave them.'

Reluctantly, Pen obeyed. She served Aunt Tribulation a large bowl of chowder and, taking some herself, began to eat it noisily.

'Don't gulp so, miss! You sound like a pig. And, talking about pigs, why are they squealing? I don't believe you can have fed them properly. Go and give them more to eat.'

While Pen was outside there was a short, sharp report from the direction of Quidnet. A twisting snake of green light shot into the twilit sky and fell, scattering sparks. Oh my goodness! thought Pen. She hurried indoors.

Aunt Tribulation was hastily putting on her bonnet.

'Oh, please, Aunt, where are you going?'

'It's none of your business, miss. Mind you wash the dishes now.'

'Oh, but please – before you go – I want to ask you how to make wedding-cake – '

'Have you gone *mad*, child? Pass my umbrella – there, by the flour crock.'

'I mean,' said poor Pen. 'Not wedding-cake, I mean, please, would you give me some advice about my sampler? I should so like to do the sails in satin-stitch, but I do not know how. Would you be so kind as to show me, and then I can sew it after I have finished the dishes?'

Aunt Tribulation looked at her narrowly. 'What's all this about? Wedding-cake – samplers – *are you concealing something from me, Penitence?*'

'N-n-no, Aunt!'

Aunt Tribulation took a menacing step towards Pen, who winced back. But just at that moment the clock struck the half hour. Aunt Tribulation appeared to recollect that time was too short for questions.

'Make haste then,' she said. 'Fetch the sampler.'

Relieved, Pen ran up to her room, unaware that Aunt Tribulation followed behind with swift, silent steps. As Pen knelt to take the canvas from its tissue in her bottom drawer, she heard the key turn in her door. She had been locked in.

Darting to the window she saw Aunt Tribulation walk into the yard and attempt to let off the damp rocket. After some struggles and furious exclamations, she finally abandoned the attempt. Putting the bundle of matches in her reticule, she set off with rapid strides for the forest.

'Be-e-e-eh!' bleated Dido in Nate's ear. 'Hallo! All rug?'

'Nearly done!' he whispered. 'We made fast, the prof's

just taking a last look. I think he can't hardly bear to say goodbye to his gun. It was lucky we'd covered the rope with leaves and bits o' brush as we went – we'd hardly finished when two of those deadbeats came sloping past going towards Sankaty; on their way to drop our poor bodies over the cliff, I reckon. Wonder what they'll do when they find we're gone?'

'Get lickety-spit to blazes outa there I should think,' guessed Dido.

She added uneasily, 'Hope they don't run up agin Cap'n Casket and the doc, though. Here's old man Breadno. All hunkydory, professor?'

'Ja. Is fastmakingness,' he said sadly.

'Then we'd better be fast making tracks. Give the signal, Nate.'

Nate gave two vigorous tugs on the rope, to indicate to Doctor Mayhew and the captain at the other end that the gun was now attached.

'Now, scarper, cullies – follow me!' Dido said. 'We want to be well away from the rope after they fix it to old Rosie, or we're liable to have our feet scorched from under us. But keep low.'

Crouching under their sheepskins they hurried over the scrubby ground as fast as they dared to the hollow where Dido had left the mule-cart. Just as Nate was untying Mungo they were surprised by the report of a rocket, and its green light climbing up the sky illuminated their startled faces as they stared at one another.

'D'you suppose that's *them*?'

'Dunno, but whatever it is, we'd best hurry,' Dido muttered. 'Give Mungo a prod, Nate.' They scrambled into the cart and Mungo, who was not used to rockets, bolted away down the track towards Sankaty. They could see the lighthouse beam clear ahead of them.

'Shouldn't be far now,' Dido said. 'Wonder when old Rosie will start? They seem to be taking a pesky long time tying the rope to her tail. Oh, *Nate* – s'pose she acts up and won't have it, and skaddles off out o' reach?'

'Nonsense,' he said more stoutly than he felt. 'She'll do anything for Cap'n Casket, eat outa his hand.'

Just before they reached the lighthouse they heard a choking, panting voice which called to them from the side of the road.

'Dido! Nate! Is that you? Oh, stop, please stop, it's Pen!'

'Why, Penny!' Dido jumped out of the cart and lifted her in. 'Are you all right, Pen? What's happened?'

'She – Aunt Trib – she's started for the forest –' gasped Penitence. 'I can't – couldn't – stop her –' She had run so far and fast that her chest was heaving painfully; she pressed both hands against it but could not speak for several moments. 'Climbed out to tell you –' she got out presently – 'rocket – meant – fire –'

'Oh, poison,' Dido said. 'That rocket was their signal, you mean?'

Pen nodded, gulping in air. The others exchanged glances of dismay at this confirmation of their fears. 'So, any minute now –' said Dido. 'Croopus, what in tarnation's Cap'n Casket –'

But as she spoke her words were drowned by a vast, prolonged, ear-shattering bellow that seemed to make even the lighthouse tremble to its foundations. They heard the rope twang like a banjo-string as the slack was suddenly drawn up. They heard a shrill whistling hiss, like the whine of wind in rigging, as the rope flew over the uneven ground, cutting through sand, slicing off shrubs and seagrass. They heard a wild shout of warning from the dory, which came in sight at this moment, Captain Casket and Doctor Mayhew rowing frantically for land. The tide was full and the waves struck at the very foot of the cliff.

'Great candles!' cried Dido. 'There she goes!'

As they strained their eyes seawards they had an instant's

glimpse of the pink whale flashing across the lighthouse beam, half out of the water, arrow-straight and wild-eyed, with her flukes streaming behind her like pennants. Then she was gone, into the dark, heading north.

'Oh *dear*!' said Pen. 'I didn't think she'd like it! Supposing she doesn't forgive us and never comes back? Poor Papa will break his heart.'

'Don't let's worry about *that* yet,' said Dido. 'He can go arter her when things has calmed down and feed her some cream buns or corn-dodgers – the main thing is, now, will the rope hold? And where's Auntie Trib?'

Two minutes later her questions were to be dramatically answered.

With a low rumbling, which increased as it approached to a clamorous clattering din, the huge gun rattled into sight, lurching over the rough ground on its innumerable pairs of wheels, tipping and swaying like a log in a torrent but, by a miracle, remaining upright. 'Look, *look*!' gasped Penitence. 'There's somebody on it!'

The light from the rising moon showed a wild figure clinging to the gun-carriage – Aunt Tribulation, astride the chassis, mad with rage, fiercely striking match after match on the breech in a last relentless effort to fire the gun as it was dragged along. Not one of the wet matches would light.

'She'll be over the cliff if she don't take care!' Nate exclaimed.

Aunt Tribulation heard him. Observing for the first time how near to the sea the gun had been dragged in its headlong course she abandoned the matches and flung them from her with a curse. Shaking her fist at the party on the cart, screaming imprecations, she leapt with frantic agility up on to the breech itself, and ran, balancing like a tightrope walker, along the barrel of the gun.

'She's got a knife!' cried Nate.

'She's going to cut the rope!'

'She'll never do it!'

'Yes she will, by thunder!'

But even as she sawed furiously at the tough five-inch manila rope there came a last crazy lurch of the gun; the muzzle dropped, the breech reared up into the sky and remained poised for an instant on the edge of the cliff – then the gun and its wild rider plunged over and down, disappearing without a sound into the white foam below.

II

*Mr Jenkins returns – the civic banquet –
the* Thrush *– another Aunt Tribulation –
goodbye to the pink whale*

DIDO woke suddenly, and lay blinking in astonishment, not quite sure where she was. The sun was blazing in at the window, and somebody was perched on her chest, repeating over and over again in a patient voice:

'Your ladyship's bath is growing cold.'

'Mr *Jenkins*!' Dido exclaimed, coming to with a jerk. 'Why, you funny old bird, how did you get here? Is the *Sarah Casket* in port, then?'

'Your Grace's wig needs a little powder,' Mr Jenkins replied. Dido jumped out of bed and began dressing. 'Wake up, Penny!' she said, thumping the mounds of quilts on the other side of the bed. 'Look who's here! Wake up, we've got visitors to cook breakfast for!'

But when they hurried downstairs they found that the visitors were already doing for themselves. Nate had been out feeding the pigs, Professor Breadno wandered in with a hatful of eggs and a heron feather, while Doctor Mayhew was scientifically thumping away at a bowl of beaten biscuit mixture.

'Look who's come!' Dido cried. Mr Jenkins left her shoulder where he had been sitting, and launched himself like a loving rocket at Nate's head, crying, 'Oh, your Excellency, I am afraid your sword has got caught in the carriage door.'

Captain Casket's eyes lit up. He had been sitting in the rocker, looking a little sad and downcast, the only member of the party to do so; but now he brightened. 'Why, Nate!

Thy bird has come back to thee! That must surely mean that the *Sarah Casket* has returned. We must set off for Nantucket town at once.'

'Ay, that we must,' Doctor Mayhew said. 'My patients will be wondering if I've gone underground. And there is much to organize – a service of thanksgiving for having been saved from Atlantic City, and a civic banquet for our noble preservers –' He chucked Pen under the chin, pulled Dido's ear, and tweaked a lock of Nate's red hair. 'Then we must send a warning about the *Dark Diamond* to the British navy. Those miscreants must be caught.'

'And I,' Captain Casket said, 'must find out the where-abouts of my sister Tribulation, in order that she may come and look after the children while I search for the pink whale.'

Penitence suddenly burst into tears.

'Why, Penny!' Dido exclaimed in concern. 'What's the matter, girl?'

'What ails thee, Daughter?'

'It's too unfair!' wept Penitence. 'I tried so hard not to be afraid of Aunt Tribulation, and now it turns out she was the wrong one and I've got to start all over again.'

'Never mind,' Dido comforted. 'The real one *couldn't* be any worse.'

After breakfast Nate hurried home to assure his mother of his safety. He found his pony straying in the forest; there was little other sign of the conspirators there, except for some broken bushes, for the gun had smashed their hut to fragments on its rush to the sea.

As soon as Nate returned they all went in to Nantucket town together and made haste to the North Wharf where the *Sarah Casket* was berthed. Great was the joy of the crew, particularly Uncle 'Lije, on seeing that Captain Casket and Nate were safe and not drowned, as had been thought.

'We reckoned as we'd make it a plum-pudding voyage,

Cap'n,' Mr Pardon said, 'and come back with only half our barrels full, for, to tell truth, when we heard the pink 'un had been sighted off Nantucket I'd half a mind to wonder whether somehow you hadn't run aground here. I'm powerful glad we did come back. Hear there's been some everlasting rum doin's in the old place since we left. Guess you'll be glad to put to sea again, Cap'n?'

'Yes, Mr Pardon,' Captain Casket said rather mournfully.

'He's pining for the pink 'un,' Dido whispered to Nate, who nodded gloomily. However they all cheered up during the civic banquet, which was indeed a splendid affair. Professor Breadno, who had struck up a friendship with Doctor Mayhew, ate so many Nantucket Wonders that he was almost consoled for the loss of his gun, while Dido, Nate and Penitence were toasted so often for their part in saving the island from disaster that they became quite bashful and retired out on to the balcony of the Grampus Inn (where the banquet was held) in order to recover their countenances. However they had not been out there more than a few minutes when Dido came flying in to exclaim:

'Doc Mayhew, do come and see, there's a British man o' war beyond the harbour bar and she's lowered a pinnace and the pinnace is a-coming into the harbour!'

'If she's looking for the plotters she's come to the wrong shop,' Doctor Mayhew said. But he slung his mayoral chain round his neck again (he had taken it off for the easier consumption of scallops) and went out to greet the captain of the English sloop *Thrush* who now came ashore, saluted, introduced himself as Captain Osbaldeston, and asked permission to make some inquiries about a gang of English criminals who were thought to be lurking on Nantucket.

'You needn't bother, sir, you needn't bother!' Doctor Mayhew told him affably. 'Mind you, so long as they'd left us alone, we'd 'a left *them* alone, and you could have saved your breath asking for them. But as we found 'em to be a nest of plaguy varmints we cleared them out ourselves, there's not one left in the island. Instead of losing time here you should be out chasing their schooner *Dark Diamond* – she's probably halfway to Land's End by now.'

'Oh no she's not,' Captain Osbaldeston corrected him. 'She's lying in a hundred fathom of water in Massachusetts Bay.'

'Eh?' exclaimed Doctor Mayhew, much startled by this information. 'How did that happen, then? How did that come about?'

Captain Osbaldeston explained. He had just abandoned his fruitless search for *Dark Diamond* on the previous evening, he said, and was about to up anchor and make for home when, shortly after moonrise, he saw a schooner scudding along the Nantucket coast under full press of sail. He thought it was his quarry.

'We were in the lee of the land at the time and she didn't appear to see us; she was coming up fairly fast when suddenly the strangest accident befell her that ever I witnessed in all my life at sea.'

'What happened?' Dido and Nate asked in one breath.

'Why, a thing that looked in the moonshine like a great pink whale came tearing along the coast, dragging behind it what seemed to be a rope. It cut clean across the schooner's course and when this rope struck the *Dark Diamond*, such was the speed of the whale's progress, if you will believe me, sir, that this rope sliced the schooner clean in two, and she sank in a matter of moments. It was an awesome sight, sir, it was indeed! Of course we searched the waters round about, but we were unable to find any survivors.'

'Then the world is well rid of a pack of trouble-makers,' Doctor Mayhew observed cheerfully. 'But won't you join our celebration, sir, since your task is at an end? Come in and drink a toast to our young friends here, who succeeded in getting rid of this nest of cockatrices for us.'

Captain Osbaldeston observed that he would be very pleased to hear the whole story leading up to the mysterious destruction of the *Dark Diamond*, so that he could include it in his report to the First Lord of the Admiralty. He came in and drank a great many glasses of ginger-jub while the tale was told.

'So this young lady is a British citizen, is she?' he inquired, looking at Dido when he had heard it all. 'Do you wish to be repatriated, madam?'

'To be whiched?'

'Would you like a passage back to England, my dear?'

Dido choked over a pickled tamarind. The temptation was almost irresistible. But she saw Pen's imploring eyes fixed on her and summoned the resolution to say, gruffly:

'That's mighty civil of you, mister, and I thank you kindly, but I guess I'd better stick in Nantucket yet awhile. I made a promise I'd stay with a friend till they was fixed up right and tight, which they ain't yet. So thanks, but not this time.'

'In that case,' Captain Osbaldeston said, 'I'd best be on my way.' And he bowed to the company and returned to his pinnace. Dido went out to watch it flit across the harbour, and to take several deep breaths and rub a slight mistiness away from her eyes. As she stood on the balcony, reluctant to go back to the gaiety of the banquet, she noticed the sails of another ship, a three-masted whaler, approaching Brant Point.

'Sail-o!' she called. 'There's a-plenty traffic today.'

The new ship, which presently revealed itself as the *Topsy Turvey*, came to anchor at length against the South Wharf, and everybody ran out to gaze at her in curiosity, for she was not a Nantucket vessel. The moment she was berthed a stout lady who stood on deck had herself slung ashore in a barrel-chair and came bustling along the wharf in a state of great excitement.

'Can anybody give me news of Captain Jabez Casket?' she asked. 'Is he 'live or drownded? – Why, there he *is*, his own self! Jabez! Brother Jabez! I declare, I never thought to see you more. I'd heard you was swallowed up by a pink whale!'

'Why, Sister Tribulation! I am amazed to see thee! Where has thee been?'

'And there's Mr Pardon! And my old friend Enoch Mayhew – ho, ho, do you remember when you pushed me in the creek, you wicked old fellow!'

'Good gracious!' whispered Pen in Dido's ear. 'Can *she* be Aunt Tribulation?'

The stout lady was cheerfully, even fashionably dressed in pink-and-grey striped sarsenet, with flounces, and a pink satin parasol, and cherries on her bonnet. She had black curls and gay black eyes, and her face was round and rosy and soft, like a pink frosted cake. She smelt strongly of lavender.

'Oh, don't call me Tribulation please, Jabez, I have quite got out of *that* habit,' she said laughing. 'Sam always calls me Topsy. Only fancy! I am married, Jabez! This is my husband, Captain Sam Turvey. We got married all of a sudden last fall, and I went off to sea with him. That was why I wrote my second letter saying that I should not, after all, be able to take care of Penitence in Nantucket. But of course when I heard you had been swallowed by the whale –'

'Second letter? But I had no second letter,' he said, bewildered.

'Did you not? I sent it to Galapagos with Captain Bilger; I made sure you'd have had it by now. But where *is* Pen, then? How have you managed?'

She turned gaily round, exclaiming, 'Now, which is my niece? Let me see if I can pick her out!'

'Here I am, Aunt Tribulation,' Pen said shyly.

'Topsy, love, Topsy! Never call me Aunt Tribulation!' cried Aunt Topsy, enveloping Pen in a warm hug. 'Yes, and I can see your mother in every inch of you but how you've grown, bless you! I'd not have known you.'

'I'd never have known *you*,' Pen murmured.

'No, *that* you wouldn't,' Dido muttered to herself, amazed at the difference between Pen's five-year-old memory of her aunt and this cheerful, pink-cheeked, sweet-scented, bustling reality. Pen's ma must have had some right silly ideas, she thought, to call her a dragon. Oh dear, why did this Auntie Trib have to go to sea? If only she'd stayed on shore, everything would have been all hunky-dory. Pen's taken a fair fancy to her, anyone can see that with half an eye.

It was true. Penitence was leaning happily in the circle of Aunt Topsy's arm, her eyes shining like stars.

'. . . so as I've decided that a life at sea doesn't suit me,' Aunt Topsy was saying, 'I'm going to stay right here in Nantucket and build me a house out at 'Sconset, for Sam to come back to between trips. And you'll keep me company there, won't you, Penny, when you Papa's at sea?'

'Oh yes!' Pen cried joyfully. 'Oh yes, Aunt Topsy!'

'Oh no!' groaned Dido involuntarily. 'Oh, why the blazes couldn't you have sailed in an hour ago instead of *now*? Then I coulda been snug aboard the *Thrush* at this very minute, a-sailing back to London River.'

'Oh, Dido!' cried Pen remorsefully. 'What a shame! But you can stay with me and Aunt Topsy till we find you another ship.'

'It's all right – never mind.' But Dido bit her lip.

Suddenly Captain Casket shook himself out of his sad reverie.

'Nay!' he exclaimed. 'But we'll up anchor with the *Sarah Casket*! A Nantucket whaler can soon overhaul that lumbering English craft. We'll put thee aboard!'

'Oh!' cried Dido. '*Could* you?'

Captain Casket was already rattling out orders: sails were shaken loose and the anchor was whisked up; half Nantucket town crowded on board to see Dido on her way.

The *Thrush* had a considerable start but was still in view, and the *Sarah Casket* rapidly began to gain on her as they crossed the Gulf of Maine. Then it could be seen that the *Thrush* was hauling her wind and bringing to; soon they saw the reason for this. Out of the north-east, arrowing through the ocean in a shower of spray like a broad piece of sunrise-coloured ribbon, came something that could only be the pink whale herself.

'It's Rosie!' Dido cried. 'It's Rosie come back to look for the cap'n!'

'Come back to see you off,' said Nate.

'Come back to forgive us,' said Pen softly.

Rosie frolicked round the *Sarah Casket* like a flying-fish, and the blue-jackets on board the *Thrush* crowded the rail to gaze in astonishment at this phenomenon.

Captain Casket hailed the *Thrush*.

'Hey, there! Can you take a passenger? Miss Twite would like to sail to England after all.'

'And welcome!' the *Thrush* replied. The captain's gig was sent across for Dido. She hugged everybody on the *Sarah Casket* goodbye. Now that she was really leaving she found herself sad; but just the same she was happy – very, very happy – to be homeward bound at last.

'Come back soon, *dear* Dido!' said Pen. 'Come and stay with me and Aunt Topsy next summer.'

'Forvandel, blisschild,' said Professor Breadno, who had accepted an invitation to stay with Doctor Mayhew and study snowy owls.

'So long!' said Nate.

'You'll always be welcome in Nantucket,' said Doctor Mayhew. 'You saved it from a fate, far, far worse than death.'

'Thee is a good child,' said Captain Casket.

'Your ladyship's carriage stops the way,' said Mr Jenkins.

Dido jumped down into the gig and was rowed across. When she reached the *Thrush* they piped her on board as if she had been the Queen herself, and the captain invited her to sit at his table. But she waited on deck, watching and waving until the *Sarah Casket*, escorted most joyfully by the pink whale, had started back to Nantucket and was out of sight.

When Dido went back next year to visit Pen she found that Captain Casket had given up seafaring. Since the pink whale had returned, his only wish was to live on Nantucket and watch her every day as she sported and frolicked off its shores.

And, as whales and sea-captains are both notoriously long-lived, it is possible that if you go to Nantucket today you may still have a sight of them.

> Dear whale of Nantucket, so pink and so round,
> The pride of our island, the pearl of the Sound,
> By Providence blest to our shores you were led,
> Long, long may you gambol off Sankaty Head!

ABOUT THE AUTHOR

Joan Aiken was born in Rye, Sussex, in 1924. Her father is the American writer Conrad Aiken, of New England and 'Mayflower' ancestry. Miss Aiken has engaged in a variety of work, including ten years with the London office of the United Nations. For five years she was a feature editor for *Argosy*, and more recently has worked as a copy-writer for a large London advertising agency. She has always written a great deal, mostly short stories, but now she devotes all her time to free-lance authorship. Her hobbies are painting and gardening at her home, an ex-pub in Petworth.

The Wolves of Willoughby Chase, Black Hearts in Battersea, The Whispering Mountain, A Small Pinch of Weather, The Cuckoo Tree, All But a Few and *The Kingdom Under the Sea* are also available in Puffins.

If you have enjoyed this book and would like to know about others which we publish, why not join the Puffin Club? You will receive the club magazine, *Puffin Post*, four times a year and a smart badge and membership book. You will also be able to enter all the competitions. For details of cost and an application form, send a stamped addressed envelope to:

The Puffin Club Dept A
Penguin Books Limited
Bath Road
Harmondsworth
Middlesex